A Small Book of Short Stories

Nick Boersema

authorHOUSE®

AuthorHouse™
1663 Liberty Drive
Bloomington, IN 47403
www.authorhouse.com
Phone: 1-800-839-8640

First published by AuthorHouse 6/9/2009

ISBN: 978-1-4389-8208-3 (e)
ISBN: 978-1-4389-8207-6 (sc)

Printed in the United States of America
Bloomington, Indiana

This book is printed on acid-free paper.

To my wife Christina.
Honey, I finally finished something that I started!...

And to Oma Boersema.
Ninety-two years is a very good age...

Contents

A New Toy

Ben had woken up one morning wanting a new four-wheeler. He had read all the articles in the latest power sports magazines. He had even browsed through the numerous lists of specifications posted on the various manufacturers' Web sites. Finally, after weeks of careful deliberation, he had made the important decision as to which four-wheeler he should own. Ben had gone down to Jake's Equipment and wandered the gleaming showroom in anticipation of his new purchase. Aisles of toys had come into focus as he stepped through the door. Ben took a deep breath, enjoying the aroma of new rubber and plastic as he browsed through the store. "Can I help you with something, sir?" asked the clerk behind the counter. He was wearing a white polo shirt with the name "Terry" embroidered on the chest in blue lettering. "Yeah," Ben replied, "I'd like a price on this red machine over here." "It's a nice ride," Terry stated. "That one will run you almost seven thousand—$6,899 to be exact." Ben swallowed hard. He looked at the red four-wheeler; it was more money than he had thought. Ben turned back to Terry. He was standing there, staring at him with an expectant look on his face. "Are you interested?" he inquired. "Yes," Ben answered. "Well, I think so— I'd better talk to the wife." "No problem," Terry told him with a wry smile. "Take your time."

Ben turned and walked out of the showroom. He got back into his old half-ton truck and pulled ahead to the edge of the parking lot. As soon as there was a break in traffic, he gunned the engine and turned onto the road. On the short drive home, Ben started wondering. *What would be the best way to present the idea of a new four-wheeler to Madison?* The $6,899 price tag was a lot of money, and she had been upset with him the last time he had spent a fraction of that amount. Maybe last time, Ben thought, it wasn't so much the amount of money he had spent, but what he had spent it on. Last time it had been nearly $400 Ben had spent, and it was on a new set of golf clubs. There had been nothing wrong with his old set of clubs—other than the fact that he had never owned any. Actually, he had never even used any if you wanted to get particular about it. To be perfectly honest, he hadn't really ever golfed in his life! Golf was something that had intrigued Ben. How could so many people spend such an incredible amount of time beating the living snot out of a little white ball? Ben had always wanted to try golf, and he had purchased those clubs with the best of intentions. *I'll schedule a golf lesson for next week*, Ben had decided, as he walked out of the store. The next week the weather was cold and rainy. *Maybe in a few days*, he had thought, and so it went on as the set of clubs continued to gather dust in the back corner of the garage. Finally, Ben had just forgotten about the clubs after winter hit.

Right now, he was pulling into his laneway without the slightest idea of how to talk to Madison about his plan of getting a new four-wheeler. Ben parked his truck along the side of the garage and went into the house through the back door. He threw his jacket on a coat hook and headed to kitchen where Madison was preparing supper. "Hi, honey," she said as Ben came into the room. "Hi," Ben replied. Before he knew it, he just blurted it out. "I want to get a new four-wheeler." Madison didn't even look up from the meal she was preparing. "Aren't they expensive?" she asked. "Well… yeah," Ben replied. "Do you think we can afford it?" inquired Madison. "Sure," he answered casually. "It might even save us money." "Just how would it do that?" Madison asked pointedly. Ben thought long and hard. How *would* a new four-wheeler save money? "Well," he said, "the one we have now is old, honey. Repairs are staring to cost us more and more. Who knows how long it will last." Madison was quiet for a moment. "I guess that makes sense," she admitted. Ben sensed a glimmer of light at the end of the tunnel. "So, what do you think?" he pressed. "I'm not entirely sure," she said. "Do we really need it? And how much will it cost, anyway?" Ben could see his glimmer of light rapidly fading. "I suppose it's not a necessity," he replied. "But I would really enjoy it." "I'm sure you would," said Madison. "How much will it cost?" she repeated. "Nearly seven thousand dollars," Ben answered carefully. He quickly added, "But if I trade in the one we have now, I'm sure it would be a lot cheaper." Madison looked up from the counter. "Just how much cheaper?" she asked. "Would it be worthwhile to trade it in, or should we just keep it?" "I don't know," admitted Ben. "But I could go back to Jake's after supper and find out," he added hopefully. Madison gazed at him from across the counter. "Back to Jake's, huh? I suppose you might have time after supper," she said, adding, "Would you mind setting the table for supper?" Ben whisked some plates from the cupboard, snatched the silverware from a drawer, and trotted off toward the dining room.

After supper Ben cleared the table and brought the dirty dishes back to the kitchen. "See you in a bit," he said, as he headed for the back door. Once outside, Ben lost no time getting into the truck and backing down the laneway. Madison watched through the kitchen window as Ben pulled away from the mailbox. The dishes could wait she decided. Madison grabbed a jacket off a coat hook in the back hall and headed out the door toward the drive shed. When she reached the drive shed, Madison spent a moment fumbling for the key. Eventually, she managed to dig the key from her pocket and slide open the door. Madison lifted her helmet from a shelf that hung off the wall, next to where the four-wheeler was parked. She slid the helmet smoothly onto her head and tugged the chinstrap tight. Madison climbed onto the four-wheeler, turned the key, and pressed the start button.

The four-wheeler came to life in an instant. Madison idled out of the drive shed, jabbed the throttle with her thumb, and tore down the laneway. She spun left, past the mailbox, and flew down the gravel road, enjoying that same freedom she felt every time she rode. Madison cruised along the road for a minute or so and then hung another left into a field. She followed the path along the fence line that lead to the woodlot behind their house. When she reached the woodlot, she slowed and chose a trail that would lead her through the bush and to the back laneway, ending up behind the drive shed. As she rode down the trail, Madison came to a clearing that had a large pond nestled in its centre. Next to the pond was the small cabin Ben had built a few years back. Madison laughed out loud as she remembered all the fun they had enjoyed with friends and family, fishing, four-wheeling, and playing pond hockey in the winter. She could still see her dad last winter, playing goal during a game of pond hockey. He had been using a snow shovel for a goalie stick. Madison's little sister Emily had taken a shot on net, only to have the puck bounce overtop of the snow shovel and hit him square in the knee! She could still hear the yelp of surprise as he had dropped the shovel and clutched his leg. "I told you that shovel was a bad idea, Dad," twelve-year-old Emily had remarked.

By now it was starting to get late. The sun was beginning to dip in the sky, so Madison decided to head back to the house. Continuing along the trail, she suddenly remembered the pile of filthy dishes waiting for her on the kitchen counter, next to the sink. She jabbed the throttle, hoping to get home and start the dishes before Ben returned from town. Madison whipped around the next corner and instantly locked the brakes. Since the last time she had ridden this trail, a tree had fallen, blocking most of the pathway. She was carrying too much speed to stop. She tried to swerve around the fallen tree but just managed to tag it with the back wheel, sending her sliding toward the edge of the trail. The four-wheeler ran through some small bushes and came to a sudden and complete stop against the base of a large maple tree. Madison took a moment to catch her breath and then slowly reversed the four-wheeler out of the trees and back onto the trail. Climbing off the machine, she checked it over for damage, starting with the wheel that had struck the downed tree. Finding nothing wrong, she moved around to the front of the vehicle. She groaned with dismay. The front bumper was pushed in at least a couple inches, and one of the headlights was cracked, pointing hopelessly up at the sky. With no other viable options, Madison decided to cut her losses and continue home.

When she got there, she found that Ben still hadn't returned. After parking the four-wheeler, Madison slid the door to the drive shed shut and locked it behind her. Once she was back inside the kitchen, she started on the stack of dishes by the sink. Before long, she saw lights coming down the road and heard Ben pull up to the house. Madison could feel a strange knot forming in her stomach—how was she going to tell him about her mishap with the four-wheeler? Would Ben be angry with her? Whisking another plate into the sink of soapy water, she scrubbed vigorously, wishing she had never gone for a ride at all. Just then, Ben came through the door with a smile on his face, whistling a cheerful tune. Madison scrubbed the dirty plate even harder. "Great news," Ben said. "The sales manager at Jake's will give me $2,000 toward a new four-wheeler if we trade our old one in." Madison replied, "That's really great, Ben." "I know," Ben continued, "At Jake's, they said it was mostly because our four-wheeler was in such great cosmetic shape that they could give us that much for it. You know, no dents or scrapes; it still looked really good the last time I brought it to them for service." Madison swallowed the lump that had formed in her throat. She could feel it twisting around as it worked its way down to meet the knot in her stomach. "Oh," was all she said. Madison worked at finishing the dishes, while Ben dug out some paperwork and sat down at the kitchen table. As Madison scoured a dirty pan, she gathered a rather small amount of courage. "Ben," she asked. "What if our four-wheeler did have some dents and scrapes? Would that really affect the trade-in value?" Ben didn't bother looking up from the stack of papers in front of him. "Yeah, it would probably make a considerable difference. I mean no one wants to buy a banged-up piece of junk, right?" "No, I guess not," said Madison. She could feel the lump she had swallowed picking up speed. Taking a deep breath, Madison said, "Ben, I have to tell you something." Ben looked up from his paperwork and grimaced. "You think buying this new four-wheeler is a bad idea don't you?" he said. "Well, not really," answered Madison as she stared into the sink of dirty water. "I was just thinking maybe we shouldn't trade in the old one." Ben stared at her with a puzzled look. "Why not?" he asked. Madison took another deep breath. "I was kind of hoping that we could go riding together sometimes. If we had two four-wheelers that is," Madison said, glancing at Ben. Smiling at her, Ben said, "I think that's a great idea, honey." Madison forced herself to smile back at him. "Also, there is something else Ben. While you were at Jake's, I took the four-wheeler out for a ride to the bush. I hit a tree. Now there's a big dent in the front bumper, and one of the headlights is broken." Ben looked startled. "Are you okay?" he asked. "I'm fine," Madison reassured him, "I just wish I could say the same for the four-wheeler. You're not angry are you?" Ben stared at her for a minute and then burst out laughing. "Of course I'm not angry," he chuckled. "The look on your face is priceless." Madison let out a sigh of relief and managed to crack a smile. Ben was still smirking at her. "I remember the first four-wheeler my family had when I was growing up," he said. "We had a track running along the entire back yard that we could ride on. I was riding one day in the rain, spinning donuts on the wet clay. There were some weeds growing along the edge of the track, hiding a big pothole. When I came sliding around the corner, my back wheel hit the pothole, and the four-wheeler rolled over." "You weren't hurt were you?" asked Madison. "No," answered Ben. "I was going fast enough that I was thrown clear, but the four-wheeler landed upside down and bent the handlebars. I flipped it back onto its wheels and let it sit for a while. After that, it started up, and I drove it back to the shed. I was so worried," Ben reminisced. "But when my dad got home from work I took him to the shed to look at the four-wheeler, and he wasn't even mad. He just had me straighten out the handlebars and told me to quit doing donuts." "Sounds like you got off pretty easy," said Madison. "Yeah, I guess sometimes stuff happens, so you just have to let it go," replied Ben. "So do you want to keep the old four-wheeler?" Madison grinned, "Absolutely. When are you going to pick up the new one?" "So you're okay with it?" Ben asked excitedly. "Sure," she replied. "It should be fun." "Tomorrow's Friday," said Ben, "I could pick it up after I close the shop." Madison yawned. "Sounds good. Let's get some sleep."

The next morning, Ben was up at his usual time. He brushed his teeth, got ready for work, and went downstairs to join Madison in the kitchen for breakfast. While they were eating, Ben said, "I'll close up the shop at five o'clock and go straight to Jake's. I should be home in time for supper." Madison smiled. "Okay, have a good day at work," she said. After breakfast they quickly cleaned up the dishes, and Ben left for town while Madison continued with his unfinished paperwork from the night before.

When Ben arrived at his shop he unlocked the front entrance and flipped the sign on the door to "Open." Ben's shop sold and installed tires. There was a large sign over the front window that read "Ben's Tire." He serviced a wide variety of customers, from farmers to construction contractors, and don't forget the everyday driver. Ben was proud of his shop. He had worked there for his uncle after school every day, all through high school, and when his uncle decided to retire a year later, he had sold the business to Ben. Now Ben ran the shop with the help of his younger brother Tim and a few co-op students from the local high school. Today Ben's mind wasn't really on his work. He went to his office and sat down in the leather chair behind his desk. He picked up the phone and started calling in orders to his suppliers. After an hour or two, Ben was sick of talking on the phone, so he went to the service bay to see what his brother was up to. "Morning, Tim," he said as he strode into the garage. "Wassup," was Tim's customary response. "Not much," replied Ben. "I think I'll go upstairs and do some inventory."

Ben headed for the stairs, and after reaching the top, he soon became busy sorting through the stacks of tires, deciding what he needed to order next. Before he knew it, lunch had rolled around, so he went back to his office to eat. While Ben was eating, his phone rang. It was one of his suppliers calling to tell him the load of tires he was expecting that afternoon had been delayed until Monday. After he was done his lunch, Ben went back to the service bay to tell Tim he would be leaving early so that he could get to Jake's sooner. Leaving instructions with Tim to close up at five, Ben went back to his office, collected his things, and headed out to the truck.

During the brief drive across town to Jake's Equipment, Ben daydreamed. He excitedly tried to imagine what it would be like to fly through the bush and across the fields on a new four-wheeler. He couldn't quite picture what riding the new machine might be like, but he was sure it would be incredible. He pulled into Jake's and headed inside to talk to the sales manager. When Ben left Jake's later, his cheque book was lighter, and his old truck was much heavier. He was proud of the brand-new, shiny four-wheeler in the back of the truck. As Ben drove, he couldn't wait to get home and show his new purchase to Madison.

Madison was out on the riding lawn mower, cutting the front yard, when Ben came wheeling into the laneway with his new toy. She went over to have a look as Ben grabbed a couple ramps from inside the drive shed. "Very nice," said Madison as Ben lowered his tailgate and set the ramps against it. "This is going to be great," he exclaimed, climbing into the back of the truck and onto the new four-wheeler. "Be careful," Madison reminded Ben as the four-wheeler rumbled to life. Ben began slowly backing down the ramps. "Don't worry," he told her. Then the machine and Ben were safely on the ground. "See, no problems. Do you want to go for a ride?" he asked Madison. "For sure!" she replied.

The Jogging Outfit

It was a Wednesday afternoon, sunny with not much wind. Madison was out running. It was her habit, twice a week, to run the country block that she and Ben lived on. Madison ran not just to keep in shape but also to relax and enjoy the beautiful countryside. As she worked her way up the next hill, she looked to her right and could clearly see the back of her house through an opening in the bush. Madison took a deep breath and charged up the remainder of the incline. When she reached the top of the hill, she took a moment to pause and revel in the gorgeous sunshine. The hill Madison was perched on top of was the part of her run that she regarded as the halfway marker. It was the end of the gradual incline she had just pushed herself through and the beginning of the slow descent that would take her back to the starting point. Madison began running again, heading for home. Soon, she was rounding the last corner and could see her mailbox at the side of the gravel road. When she got to the end of the laneway, she stopped to grab the mail from the box before continuing on to the house. Madison let herself in through the back door, leaving the mail on the kitchen counter on her way upstairs. She quickly climbed out of her sweaty running outfit and proceeded to the bathroom for a quick shower.

After showering, Madison slid into a pair of comfy old jeans, slipped on a white tank top, and went downstairs toward the kitchen. She opened the freezer and dug around until she found a casserole, which she whisked into the oven for supper. Then she turned her attention to the mail she had abandoned on the counter. Madison sorted out the bills, placing them beside the coffee maker, and began leafing through the many advertisements. As she browsed through the flyer from a local sporting goods store, a picture of a jogging outfit caught her eye. The outfit, which was available in a wide variety of colours, was made up of a sports bra with matching shorts. Both pieces of the outfit were made from the same elastic material, which Madison noted looked quite comfortable and very capable of keeping things in their proper place while one was running. The ad promised unmatched comfort and support as well as being able to wick away sweat, keeping you dry as you exercised. Madison was impressed. She tried to imagine how it would feel to go running in such an outfit. *Maybe I could go look at it tomorrow after I do groceries*, she thought. Madison put away the mail and started making a salad to go along with the casserole for supper. As she was putting the finishing touches on the salad, she heard Ben's old truck come rolling down the gravel laneway and stop next to the drive shed. Soon enough, Ben came in through the back door, whistling cheerfully as he usually did when all was right with the world. "Hi, honey," he said as he headed to the fridge for a beer. "How'd your day go?" "Good," Madison said with a smile. "We have such nice weather so I went for a run. What did you do today?" Ben grinned back at her. "Oh, not too much. It was kind of slow, so I tidied up around the shop and caught up on some inventory. Tomorrow we have another shipment of tires coming, so I'll have to get there early to help the driver unload." Madison nodded. "Sounds like you'll be busy tomorrow," she said. "Yeah, I should be," Ben replied. "Well, that's a good thing," answered Madison as she took some plates from the cupboard and began setting the table. "Why don't you go take a shower and get changed," she suggested. "By then the food should be ready and we'll eat." "Okay, sounds good," said Ben, heading upstairs.

After supper was finished, Ben helped Madison clear the table and then reached into the fridge for another beer and went outside to begin cutting the back lawn. As Ben entered the drive shed, he noticed one of the front tires on the mower was flat. "Great," Ben muttered under his breath. The weather had been rainy for the last few days, and he was anxious to keep up with the mowing before the grass got too long. Heaving a sigh, he took a deep swig from the brown bottle in his right hand. Ben took a moment to let loose a carefully composed belch, enjoying the loud echo as it resounded off the walls of the shed. Then he rolled the air compressor a little closer and started filling the tire. Once the tire was full, he disconnected the air hose and heard a hissing noise. Within a minute, the tire was flat again and the rim was resting on the shed floor. Ben found his jack in the corner of the shed and wheeled it over to the mower. He pumped it up, raising the tire off the concrete floor. Next, he took the inner tube out of the tire and brought it over to the workbench, intent on finding the hole and patching it. As he was working, Madison came walking into the shed. "I thought you were going to mow," she said. "I was," Ben replied, shooting a disgruntled look toward the mower. "But one of the tires was flat, so I'm fixing it first." "C'mon," Madison said. "You don't have to do that right now. I built a campfire and set out the lawn chairs by it. Let's go sit out by the fire and have a relaxing evening." "All right," Ben answered. "Just let me get this tube patched and back in the tire." "Sure. I'll go get us something to drink," Madison told him. "Great," Ben replied. "I'll see you in about ten minutes." Madison headed back to house to get the drinks she had promised, while Ben finished the task of patching the tube—along with the rest of his beer. Once the glue was dry, he inserted the tube back into the tire and reseated the tire on the rim. Once again, Ben put the air hose to the tire and filled it. This time it stayed full. He lowered the jack and wheeled it back into the corner where it belonged and went to join Madison by the fire.

The next morning Ben and Madison got up early and made a breakfast of bacon and fried eggs on toast, with a grapefruit on the side. Ben quickly polished off his portion of the meal and gulped down some orange juice. Then he sat there, sipping a mug of coffee and watched Madison as she ate. "Why do you always do that?" Madison asked him. "Do what?" Ben responded slowly. "Watch me while I'm eating!" Madison said, glaring at him. Ben shrugged his shoulders. "I don't know... something to do I guess." "Just quit it," Madison replied. "You're making me nervous." Ben glanced at her with a smirk on his face. "How could that make you nervous?" he asked. Madison glared at him again, scowling for good measure. "I don't know," she said. "It just does." Ben stifled a chuckle. "Well then," he said with a condescending air. "In that case, I completely understand." "Why do you have to tease me?" asked Madison as she plunged her spoon into the pink grapefruit in front of her. The grapefruit erupted with a blast of stinging juice that found a home in Ben's eye. He grunted with surprise and began to rub his eye in an attempt to rid himself of the pain. Now it was Madison's turn to smirk. "That's what you get. Don't worry, you deserved it," she remarked smugly.

Once Ben had left for work, Madison went back to bed for a couple hours. When she woke up, she got dressed and went downstairs to tidy up the kitchen. After she was done cleaning the kitchen, Madison made some room in the fridge for the groceries she was planning to pick up. She poured herself a cup of coffee, which she slowly savoured before heading out to the car. Soon she was cruising down the back roads on her way to the supermarket, singing along with the radio at the top of her voice. When she reached town and pulled up to a red light, Madison was still singing like she was on tour. She pulled out all the stops, even managing to play a few chords on her air guitar. Once the song had ended, Madison looked over at the car next to her and saw a lady staring back at her, with an expression of wild amusement on her face. Madison turned bright red and fixed her gaze on the traffic lights across the intersection. As soon as the lights turned green, she tromped on the gas pedal and took off, tires squealing through the intersection. *How embarrassing*, she thought. What if it had been somebody she knew? Madison took a deep breath as she turned the corner into the supermarket. She quickly parked the car and strode across the parking lot to the entrance of the store, grabbing a cart as she went through the automatic doors. Madison made it halfway down the first aisle before she stopped. She had her purse with her, but her wallet was still in the car.

Madison left her cart in the aisle and went back outside to get her wallet. When she reached the car, she began rummaging in her purse looking for her keys. Where were they? Frantically, she dumped the contents of her purse onto the hood of the car and began sorting through it. A feeling of dread crept up on her. Madison looked through the driver's window and saw her keys dangling from the ignition. Perfect. Just what she needed right now. She shovelled the pile of miscellaneous items off the hood and back into her purse. *Maybe*, she thought, *the car isn't locked.* Trying the door handle, she discovered it definitely was locked. Reaching into her purse, Madison pulled out her cell phone and scrolled through the directory. Eventually, she found the listing for the automobile association. She selected the number from the list and hit talk. The phone rang briefly, and a woman answered. Madison explained her situation to the woman, who asked for her location and the number on her membership card. "I don't know what the number is," she admitted, once she had given out the information regarding her whereabouts. "I locked my wallet in the car with my keys." "That's okay, dear," the woman informed her. "You can give the number to the driver once he unlocks your car. He should be there in twenty minutes." Madison breathed a sigh of relief. "Thanks so much," she said. "No problem, that's what we're here for," replied the woman as she hung up the phone.

Madison waited by the car until the tow truck showed up. In less than five minutes, the driver had opened her door, jotted down her information, and left. Madison quickly collected her keys and wallet, and headed back into the store to finish her shopping. Soon, she came back out of the store pushing a cart full of groceries. After she loaded the groceries into the trunk, she took a glance across the plaza and saw a sporting goods store. It was the same store that had advertised the jogging outfit in the flyer she had been browsing through the day before. Madison closed the trunk, carefully making sure that the keys were in her hand, and began walking over to the sports store.

When Madison walked back out of the store she was the proud owner of a bright red jogging outfit. As she started the car and began to make her way home, she was eagerly anticipating the next time she would run. Madison was nearly back at the house when she drove up behind a woman who was out for a run. The woman, she noticed, was somewhat on the larger half of the scale. Madison also noticed that the woman was wearing a pair of jogging shorts identical to the pair she had just purchased. The shorts did not look even the least bit flattering on the woman. In fact, it looked as if she had been poured into them. Madison likened the image of the woman running to that of a bag of small potatoes crammed into a cotton tube sock. Figuratively speaking, the sock was bulging at the seams. Suddenly a thought hit her. What if the outfit didn't look good on her either? She had tried it on quickly at the store but had been in a hurry and wasn't too concerned at the time. Now it worried her. As soon as the car came to a halt in her laneway, she snatched the bag containing the jogging outfit from the seat beside her. Leaving the groceries in the trunk, she ran inside to try it on. Madison walked over to the mirror, wearing the new suit. She felt a wave of relief wash over her as she stared at her reflection. She liked how the outfit looked on her. In fact, Madison thought the bright red material complemented her dark brown hair quite well. She loved the jogging outfit.

Madison loved the jogging outfit so much, that when Ben came home from work, she was in the kitchen, still wearing it. "Whoa, *I like,*" said Ben as he walked into the house. "Thank you," replied Madison. "I just picked it up today." Ben put his lunch pail on the kitchen counter. "I'm going to take a shower. By the way," he said as he headed for the bathroom, "last week I put a spare car key in one of those magnetic boxes. It's under the car on the driver's side." The kitchen echoed with the sound of Madison's hand meeting her forehead.

Night on the Town

Ben was cruising along the back roads on his way home from work. It had been a long, busy day at the tire shop. He had been run off his feet selling and installing tires. His brother Tim hadn't been feeling well and had gone home at lunchtime, leaving Ben to fend for himself as he dealt with customers and managed the co-op students. Now, as Ben drove along toward home, he reached over and flicked on the radio. The music began to relax him as he listened. He couldn't wait to get home to Madison and a cold beer. The truck's speakers began to crackle. *That's odd*, Ben thought. He always had perfectly clear reception on this station. He fiddled with the radio, trying to coax some clear music from the speakers. The radio gave one last defiant roar of static and quit altogether. *Lovely*, thought Ben. At least he was almost home. A few minutes later, he was pulling up to the house. Ben parked the truck and went inside to see Madison. "Hey, honey," she said as he walked into the kitchen and gave her a kiss. "Hi," Ben replied gloomily. "What's the matter?" asked Madison, noticing the sour expression on his face. "I'm not entirely sure," said Ben, with a hint of frustration. "The radio in my truck isn't working. It quit on the way home. I think it might have died." "I'm sorry, honey," said Madison. "I'll tell you what. I didn't feel like making supper tonight, so I thought we'd go into town and eat out. Maybe afterward we could go shopping for a new radio for your truck. What do you think?" she asked, looking at him intently. "Yeah, I guess that could work," Ben answered slowly. "Great," she said, "C'mon, we'll take my car.

Ben and Madison drove into town and went to a family-style restaurant that prided itself on a wide variety of appetizers. As they walked in the front door of the restaurant, they were greeted by a pleasant young hostess, who led them to a quiet booth off in the corner. Once they were seated, the hostess handed them a couple of menus and informed them that a waitress would be taking their orders shortly. Ben took a moment to briefly survey his surroundings. "Wow," he said. "They've made some nice changes since the last time we were here." "I can see that," replied Madison as she glanced around the restaurant. "It really does look great."

They browsed through their menus for a few minutes, considering their options. Soon a waitress appeared, asking if she could start them with some drinks. "I think I'll just have a glass of water," said Madison. "And for you, sir?" the waitress asked Ben. "I guess I'll have an iced tea," he said. "Okay, great. I'll be back with your drinks in a minute," replied the waitress before bustling off toward the kitchen. "Well, I'm all set to order," said Madison, closing her menu and placing it on the edge of the table. "I don't really know what I feel like," said Ben. "Why don't you try the rib and wing combo?" Madison asked him. "You usually enjoy something like that." Ben was slowly perusing the menu. "Not tonight." he said. "I don't think I'm in the mood for that much meat. Maybe I'll try their appetizer sampler." Madison nodded in approval. "Good choice, you can never go wrong with the sampler."

Just then the waitress arrived with their drinks. "Are we ready to order?" she asked with a smile. "Yes," replied Madison. "I would like the french onion soup and the fajita platter." "With the soup to start?" asked the waitress as she scribbled in her notepad. "Sure," said Madison. "Perfect," replied the waitress, turning to Ben. "What can I get for you?" "I'd like the appetizer combo," he said, handing her his menu. "Okay," said the waitress as she whisked Madison's menu from the table. "Your food will be out shortly."

After she left with their order, Ben turned to face Madison. "So my drive home wasn't that great," he said. "How was your day?" She smiled at him. "It was pretty good…" Her smile got wider, showing off her white teeth. "I got a part-time job at the daycare where my friend Carrie works. There was an opening, and she recommended me to her manager. Isn't that great?" Ben's expression was one of surprise. "Wow," he managed. "That's… really exciting. A daycare, huh?" "Yes," bubbled Madison. "You know I just love kids; it'll be a lot of fun. And it's only two days a week, so I'll still have lots of time to keep up around the house. Besides, we can always use some extra money, right?" "Well yeah, sure," answered Ben. "I know you've been thinking about something like this for a while now, so if this is what you want to do, then I'm proud of you. Madison grabbed Ben's hand. "I'm so glad you understand," she said.

The waitress came by with Madison's french onion soup. "Here's your soup. Enjoy!" she announced, placing the steaming bowl in front of her. Madison glanced down at the soup as the fresh aroma teased her senses. She noticed the cheese floating on top of the soup was not melted. "Look at the cheese," she said to Ben. "What's up with that? It's not even melting." The bowl was steaming hot, but the cheese did not seem to want to melt. Ben frowned at the soup as it sat across the table from him. He signalled the waitress to come back, and when she did, he explained the situation with the cheese, asking her to take the soup back and have the cheese melted. The bowl of soup was taken away and very quickly returned with the cheese nicely melted. Madison thanked the waitress as she picked up her spoon and tried the soup. "Mmmm," she said to Ben. "It's *so* good." Ben grinned. "I would hope so after all that hassle." "Oh, it wasn't that bad," said Madison. "It just took a minute." "Yeah, I guess," replied Ben, as the rest of their food was brought to the table. He quickly dug in, talking to Madison between mouthfuls.

"So, you said your friend Carrie got you the job?" he asked her. "Isn't she the one whose pets keep dying or running away?" "Yes, that's her," Madison replied. "What are you trying to get at?" "Nothing much," said Ben. "I was just wondering... if she can't even look after her pets properly, what's she doing working at a daycare?" Madison crinkled her nose at Ben. "That's not fair to Carrie," she said. "It's not her fault. If pets want to run away, you can't stop them." "Maybe not," answered Ben. "What about the ones that died though? I'm pretty sure it was her fault then." Madison stared at him. "What do you mean? How was it her fault?" Ben smirked. "Well, let's see. She went away on vacation for a month and forgot to feed her fish. When she got back, they were floating belly up!" "That could have happened to anyone," Madison said. "People just forget things; it's normal." "Okay," said Ben. "Her dog, Barney. She ran him over, backing the car out of the garage." Madison glared at him. "Barney was sleeping behind the car. Carrie couldn't see him lying there. It probably happens all the time. Besides, Barney didn't die. The vet fixed him up almost good as new." "Fine," said Ben. "I'll give you that, but what about her cat Whiskers? Carrie ran him over with a snowblower while she was clearing out her laneway. I might be going out on a limb here, but I don't think there was much left of that poor cat for the vet to work with. You would have needed a forensics team just to find the pieces," he said with a chuckle. "That's disgusting," retorted Madison. "I'm trying to eat here. Please don't tell that gross story when I'm eating; it bothers me." Ben just laughed. "If it bothers you, how do you think the cat felt?"

Soon, they finished their meal and left the restaurant. "I'll drive," said Ben as they walked across the parking lot to their car. They got into the car, and Ben started the engine. Once the dash came to life, he took a glance at the clock. "Whoa, I had no idea it was this late already. We'd better hurry up and get over to car audio place before they close." Ben put the car in gear and peeled out of the parking lot. As they turned onto the street, the traffic lights at the next intersection turned orange. Ben floored the gas pedal, just managing to fly through the intersection before the lights turned decidedly red. "We're not that late," remarked Madison. "You don't have to drive like an idiot. Besides, the store is just around the corner." Ben backed off the accelerator somewhat. Madison looked over at the speedometer. "You're still going pretty fast," she said. "You'd better slow down or you'll get a ticket." Ben shrugged off the warning and kept driving. Madison was silent for a few minutes. "Fine," she commented. "Don't listen to me. See if I care." Ben took the curve into the store parking lot as if he were in a race, found a parking spot, and shut off the car. "The keys," said Madison. "I'm driving home."

Inside the store, Ben walked over to a wall that was filled with car radios and began searching for something that would be suitable for his truck. Madison asked him, "What kind of radio do you want?" Ben looked around carefully. "The radio that's in the truck now is so old it only plays tapes. All I really want is something basic that can play CDs; it doesn't have to be really fancy." After a bit more looking, Ben found exactly the radio he wanted. Almost any radio in the store could play CDs, and the one he chose was just about the cheapest. A salesman came over to unlock the storage case and slid out a box containing the radio that Ben had chosen. "You'll need a wiring harness and a mounting kit for your dash," he told Ben. "What's the model and make of the vehicle this is going into?" Ben supplied the man with the information, and he and Madison were soon walking out of the store with the new radio. They got back into the car, this time with Madison behind the wheel, and started for home.

As they were driving, Madison began telling Ben more about her new job. She was so excited to talk about the daycare and how much fun she thought it would be, that she wasn't really paying attention to her driving. When the car reached the outskirts of town, she was clipping along at a nice country speed, which really didn't seem to match the speed limit of the town she hadn't quite left yet. Or so it seemed to the driver of the car behind her. Suddenly, Madison's mirrors were filled with bursts of red and blue lights. She quickly brought the car to a halt on the shoulder of the road as she muttered under her breath. Ben was quiet. Madison found her license and registration and rolled down her window as the officer came walking up to her window.

When the police cruiser pulled away, Madison had received her license and registration back and was the new owner of a bright yellow piece of paper. According to the note on the backside of the ticket, she had fifteen days to either pay her fine of $138.47 or book a court date and go before a judge. She turned to look at Ben. He was still quiet, but she knew he was about to burst at the seams. The gleeful look on his face said everything. The remainder of their drive home was long and quiet.

At the breakfast table the next morning, Ben was working steadily at emptying the plate in front of him. He paused every now and again to steal a glance at Madison, who seemed more interested in torturing the food on her plate than actually consuming it. Ben winced as Madison's fork impaled a piece of ripe cantaloupe. Her fork seemed to dance back and forth between the portions on her plate without actually emptying it. Ben filled a cup with coffee and handed it across the table to Madison before pouring himself a cup. "How'd you sleep, honey?" he asked her, attempting to start a conversation. "Fine, just fine," she answered. Ben decided to try again. "Did you have any plans for today?" he asked. "Not really," Madison replied sourly. "It's Saturday, so I'll probably just clean the house." "I was kind of hoping to get that new radio installed in the truck," remarked Ben. "Tim said he was feeling better, so he should be able to handle things at the shop by himself for half a day. I don't think I'll bother going in to work today." "Suit yourself," said Madison. "So... when do you think you'll be starting at the daycare?" Ben asked her, warily. "Probably early next week," she answered. "They should call on Monday to let me know."

Once the meal had come to a close, Ben stood up from the table. "I'm going to take a look at that radio in the truck and see if I can't get it switched with the new one," he said. "But it sounds like your new job will work out pretty well." "Pretty well?" asked Madison. "What does that mean?" "Well," said Ben with a smirk as he headed toward the back door, "the extra money might come in handy if you're planning on collecting anymore speeding tickets." A juicy piece of cantaloupe flew past his ear, leaving a well-defined skid mark on the wall. Ben quickly snagged a sweater from the hook on the wall and tugged the door shut behind him. The smirk never left his face as he chuckled all the way to the truck.

With Ben out of the way, Madison grumpily began the task of clearing the table and washing the dishes. As she slid dish after filthy dish in and out of the soapy water, she gradually began to feel better. Once she got into a rhythm, the dishes almost seemed to clean themselves. In a short amount of time, she had the dish rack piled full and was draining the sink. She was in the middle of drying the contents of the rack when she heard a strange noise coming from outside the back door. At first she ignored it, but eventually her curiosity got the better of her. Tossing the dish towel onto the counter, Madison went to investigate the sound. When she got to the door, the noise became noticeably louder. She opened the door and was startled when something furry darted through her legs and into the house. Madison swung around just in time to see a striped tail disappear around the corner. She ran back to the kitchen, trying to catch a glimpse of the varmint that had invaded her home. Looking around the kitchen she saw nothing. Where had it gone? Another thought occurred to her suddenly. What if it was dangerous? Whatever it was, the animal might have rabies, she realized. Maybe she should go get Ben. Madison quickly shoved that thought aside. Ben would probably just laugh at her and find the whole situation entirely too amusing, she decided. Besides how bad could it be? All she really had to do was find the unwelcome creature and help it change its mind about coming to visit her unannounced.

Madison picked up a broom from beside the fridge and advanced toward the living room, holding the broom in front of her as if it were a weapon. She carefully stepped into the living room but still saw nothing. Out of the corner of her eye, Madison detected some movement. She looked quickly to her right and spotted the striped tail sticking out from beneath the couch. Very quietly, Madison crept across the room until she was able to reach the furry tail with the broom. She stood there for a moment, trying to survey the situation. The tail she saw protruding from under the couch looked very much like that of a cat, she thought. Madison decided that the best course of action would be to poke the tail with the head of the broom and hopefully get the animal out from underneath the couch. She took a deep breath and poked.

The tail, and whatever it belonged to, exploded from its hiding spot and tore across the room, clawing its way up the heavy drapes that surrounded the large bay window. Madison had guessed right: it was certainly a cat, a good-sized cat to be sure, and it was just as certainly shredding its way up her drapes. She closed in on the cat, swinging the broom at the drapes just below were the intruder was hanging, hoping to knock it loose. It took her a couple swings, but the cat eventually loosened its hold on Madison's drapes. It dropped to the back of a nearby recliner and sprinted out of the room and into the kitchen, hissing as it went. By the time she had dashed back into the kitchen, all Madison could see was the cat's rump disappearing up the stairs to the second storey of the house.

Ben strolled through the back door and into the kitchen with the intention of refilling his coffee mug. Standing there in front of him was Madison, broom in hand and breathing rather heavily. She had a frazzled look on her face. "Wow," said Ben, topping off his mug with fresh coffee. "You just never stop cleaning do you? Why don't you go upstairs and lie down for a while? You look a bit tired; some rest might be good for you. "That sounds nice," she replied. "I think I just might do that." "Great, I'll be outside with the truck if you need me," said Ben, heading back outside. *Poor girl*, he thought as he sauntered past their inground swimming pool and over to the truck, *she must really be upset about that speeding ticket to be cleaning like that.*

As soon as the door closed in Ben's wake, Madison reaffirmed her clutch on the broom and scrambled upstairs in search of the rogue feline. When she got to the top of the stairs, she ground to a halt with a look of dismay written across her pretty features. Scattered across the hallway were miniscule chunks of shredded toilet paper. The soft tissue was strewn about as if a bomb filled with confetti had gone off, blanketing the hallway with a layer of white. Glancing around the corner into the bathroom, Madison noticed that the stand where she kept the spare toilet paper had been knocked over, and its contents were missing. There had been at least three rolls left on the stand last time she checked, and now they had been destroyed and lay out in the hall, desecrating her clean carpet.

Madison was slowly turning an odd shade of red. In fact, the longer she stared at the mess covering her hallway floor, which had only a short time before been so clean, the more it offended her sense of cleanliness. The more offended she became, the deeper shade of red her face acquired. Right now it could easily be considered an intense crimson. Madison stalked across the hall, following the trail of violated toilet paper through her bedroom doorway. What met her eyes was hard to believe.

There was the cat that had so adequately been terrorizing her house sound asleep on the bed, with its overwhelmingly hairy body curled into a tight ball. The cat was not just on the bed, it was actually lying on her pillow, infesting it with a generous layer of dander. Madison bit her lip, nearly causing it to bleed. She cast a withering gaze on the cat. She was now thoroughly upset. A strange cat was sleeping on her pillow. She wanted, more than anything else at this moment, to scream and hurl the broom in her grasp directly at the sleeping animal, with all the power and accuracy of a javelin. As she stood at the foot of the bed, wishing she could strangle the beast that was passed out in front of her, an exciting thought came to mind. It wasn't the sort of idea she would usually contemplate, but in Madison's opinion, it seemed more than suitable for the situation at hand. She moved from the foot of the bed over to the open window, with all the stealth of a navy seal. From this point, she took a moment to summarize what lay before her outside. It was a bright sunny day; the glistening blue pool below her was reflecting light in every direction imaginable. Madison smiled. It was a smile of anticipation. Silently, she unclipped the fasteners that were holding the screen in place, and removed it from the window. Next, she slid over to the bed, ever so carefully, and very gently grasped the edges of the pillow that supported the napping hooligan. In one lightning quick motion, Madison swung her arms in the direction of the open window as hard as she possibly could.

Ben had made little progress in trying to remedy the problem with his old radio. He hadn't even managed to loosen the plastic trim surrounding it, much less remove it and install the new one. This was a harder task than he had imagined. Heaving a deep sigh, he raised his coffee mug to his lips. Nothing. Not even a drop was left in the clay mug. Another sigh. Taking the mug with him, Ben trudged back to the house. As he rounded the corner to the back entrance, he was surprised to hear an agonized yowl. Instantly looking up, he saw a flailing cat sail through the air with a good deal of speed, landing with an impromptu splash in the swimming pool. The coffee mug slipped from his fingers, shattering as it hit the walkway.

Visiting Grandparents

It was the end of Madison's second day working her new job at the daycare in town. The day was a Wednesday. She had just gotten home and in the door when the phone rang. When she answered the phone, Madison was surprised to hear her grandmother's voice on the far end of the line. Her grandparents, from her mother's side of the family, lived a few hours away, nestled in the suburbs of a large city. They were well-known throughout Madison's family for their chronic inability to get along with one another. "Grandma, wow, how are you?" Madison asked. "Ben and I haven't seen you and Grandpa since last Christmas." "Oh, not bad, not bad," Grandma replied briskly. "You've been keeping well I trust. Anyways, your grandfather and I were talking the other night, and Ben and yourself came up in our conversation." Madison's grandmother never beat around the bush; she always went straight to the point. Grandma continued, "Grandpa was saying how cooped up and bored he feels, stuck in this crowded city all the time, and quite frankly, I suppose I might feel the same way. It's not often we both agree on something, so we thought we might like to get away, out to the countryside for a few days. Naturally, you and Ben were the first people we thought of." Grandma paused for a quick breath of air before rattling on. "So what do you think? Could I come visit you for a little while?" "Of course, Grandma," Madison said pleasantly. "You guys are always welcome. When were you thinking of coming?" "How does tonight sound?" asked Grandma quickly. "Your grandfather and I are already on the way. We left about an hour ago, so we should arrive at your place shortly after supper. Will that work for you and Ben?" Madison was quiet for a second, a little taken aback. "Um… sure, that should be fine," she heard herself reply, hesitantly. "Fabulous," was her grandmother's response. "Be a love and have the coffee ready for just after supper. *Earl*!" Grandma yelled into the phone. "How many times must I tell you to keep your eyes on the road? Are you trying to get us killed? After all your years of driving, one would think you'd have managed to grasp this one simple concept. Honestly, did you forget to take your medication today? You're simply all over the road."

Madison flinched at the sudden outburst, moving the receiver a safe distance from her ear so as not to become deafened. Even with the phone positioned well away from her, she could still hear Grandma's indignant tirade with stunning clarity. "Quit tailgating that truck, Earl! He's got his brake lights on, can't you see that? Where are your glasses? You know you shouldn't be driving without them; you're blind as a bat!" Madison could just make out her grandfather's muttered retort. "Keep your shirt on woman! How often have I told you to leave me alone when we're in the car? Huh? That's right, more times than I care to remember. My eyes might not be that great, but right now I wish it were my ears that didn't work!" Madison rolled her eyes. Her grandparents could never seem to stop harassing each other. Assuming that the verbal jousting in the car would continue for some time, she simply placed the phone back in the cradle and began making preparations for their arrival.

The door had barely closed behind Ben when he returned home from work, and Madison was already filling him in on the details of their impending visitors. "She just called *now* and said they were on the way?" asked Ben. "Isn't that kind of short notice?" Madison answered matter of factly, "Of course it's short notice, but what was I supposed to say? They were already in car for almost an hour. I couldn't just tell them to turn around and go home. Besides, we haven't seen them since the holidays, and it's not like we have any real plans for the next little while anyway." "Yeah, I suppose," said Ben. "But what are they going to do here for two or three days?" "I don't have to work for the rest of the week," said Madison. "I'm sure we'll find lots to do." Ben looked wary. "As long as they don't run out of things to keep themselves occupied," he said. "You know how they get when they're bored." Madison thought back to the phone conversation she had just taken part in and grimaced.

For supper, Ben took a couple of thick, juicy steaks outside and laid them on the grill. Meanwhile, inside the house, Madison boiled some corn on the cob and threw together a nice salad. When the steaks were done to perfection, Ben shut off the grill and brought them inside to the table. Once the corn was done, they filled their plates, bowed their heads, and then dug in. The meal was a quiet one, both of them realizing that they might not enjoy a meal like this until after their prospective houseguests were gone. The food had no sooner been finished and removed from the table, when a car was heard rolling down the laneway. "The coffee!" shouted Madison, lunging over to the counter and preparing the coffeemaker for a quick brew. Outside, the sound of car doors could be heard. The coffee was barely starting to drip when the doorbell rang. "Could you get the door, Ben?" Madison asked with a look of desperation. "Sure, honey," Ben answered, summoning his courage and heading toward the front door. He was halfway to his target when the door opened and Grandma came barrelling into the hall. "Ben," she cried. "How lovely to see you! My bags are in the car, be a dear and give Grandpa a hand with them, will you? Madison!" she bubbled, dashing past him into the kitchen. "You never change, do you? Still pretty as ever." Madison smiled. "You don't look too bad yourself, Grandma." "Oh, nonsense," the older lady replied. "I declare, the car ride down here must have taken five years off my life." "You promise?" growled Grandpa, appearing in the front hall, heavily laden with their luggage. "I wish I had taken my earplugs with me. Then at least one of us could have enjoyed the drive."

A short time later, after the luggage had been stowed away in the downstairs guest bedroom, the four of them sat in the living room, sipping away casually at steaming cups of coffee. "So, Ben," piped up Grandpa. "How's business at the shop?" "Right now it's pretty decent," said Ben, smiling. "I'm hoping to pick up a contract with the county for all their construction and maintenance equipment." "Excellent," replied Grandpa. "I hope that works out for you." "And Madison," he continued. "I've been hearing some rumours from your parents about you working at a daycare. How's that going so far?" "You know what Grandpa?" Madison said. "It's great. I just love it. Working with all those kids is a lot of fun. Besides, it's only a couple days a week, so I still have plenty of free time." "You know what I would just love?" asked Grandma. "A nice, cozy campfire out in the backyard. How about it?" "Oh, that sounds great," said Madison. "Come on, Ben, let's build a fire. We'll set out the lawn chairs and make s'mores. "Now you're talking," Grandpa declared. "Get me a roasting stick."

Madison and Grandma brought out the required ingredients for producing s'mores and set some lawn chairs around the fire pit. Grandpa had tagged along with Ben to the drive shed. Soon, he returned on Ben's four-wheeler with a small trailer full of split wood in tow. "These things are a hoot," he crowed, climbing off the side of the machine. "Wilma," he said, addressing his wife, "we're going for a ride tomorrow. Over to the bush back there," he rambled, waving his arms excitedly. "They've got a little rowboat over there that we can take out for a spin." Grandma looked hesitant. "I suppose that would be fine," she replied. "But only if you behave yourself on that machine. I do not want to be making any more trips to the hospital. You're not as spry anymore as you once were." "Wait a minute," Madison interjected. "*Any more trips to the hospital? When was the first trip?*" Grandpa glared across the fire pit at her grandmother. "Now see what you've done?" he grumped. "You can never leave well enough alone." "Oh, shush, Earl, you old grouch," Grandma responded as she turned to Madison. "Last winter, our neighbour got his car stuck in the snowbank along his driveway. Your grandfather was out there for at least an hour, pushing and shovelling until they had the car free again. When he got back into the house, he almost passed out on my clean kitchen floor. Naturally, I took him to the hospital to get him checked out by a doctor." "Who said there was *nothing* wrong with me," Grandpa emphasized triumphantly. "Be that as it may," Grandma went on, "he did say that since you're getting older, you need to slow down a bit." "That's hogwash, plain and simple. I'm in perfect shape," Grandpa declared.

"You know I've always said that doctor was a quack. Now it's become obvious!" Grandma just rolled her eyes.

The next morning at 9 o'clock, Ben and Madison were still in bed. The same could not be said for their visitors. Grandpa had gotten up at the crack of dawn and had left on the four-wheeler, dragging his wife with him. Madison finally crawled out of bed and made her way down to the kitchen. She found a hastily scrawled note from her grandfather lying on the counter.

Madison, your grandmother and I took the four-wheeler over to the bush. Don't bother to hold breakfast for us. We'll look after ourselves when we get back. Hope we didn't wake you and Ben. Grandpa

Madison read the last part of the note in disbelief. *Hope we didn't wake you and Ben.* The only way she and Ben could have slept through the ruckus that had gone on earlier that morning would have involved both of them being severely deaf. How she wished that had been the case. Her grandparents had been rummaging around the kitchen at half past six that morning, giving each other advice on how to work the coffeemaker. Neither one of them was capable of receiving the other's well-intentioned ideas in a gracious manner. Because of this, the nattering had quickly degraded into a two-way barrage of sarcastic comments. The debate had finally ended when the coffeemaker took it upon itself to embark on its regularly scheduled program, producing a pot of fresh coffee. Once the din in the kitchen had ceased, it was quickly transferred to the great outdoors. Grandpa had pulled the four-wheeler out of the drive shed, waiting for Grandma to climb aboard, before jabbing the throttle and hurtling off toward the bush. The piercing shriek that followed was easily heard in Ben and Madison's bedroom.

Madison cracked some eggs into a cast iron skillet, threw a few sausage links in beside the eggs, and placed the heavy skillet on the stove overtop of a cheerful flame. As soon as the aroma of sizzling meat reached the upstairs, a groggy Ben came stumbling down from the bedroom to find a place at the table. "Do your grandparents always make that much noise?" he mumbled sleepily. "I sure hope not," was Madison's reply.

The four-wheeler came rolling through the trees and reached a stop at the edge of the pond. Climbing off the machine, Grandpa and Grandma paused for a moment to take in all of their vibrant surroundings. "I just love the colour of the trees," she declared. "Yes, that is nice I suppose," he replied, "but what about the quiet? It's so peaceful back here. I only wish it was this quiet back in our neck of the woods." "I couldn't agree with you more," said Grandma. "Come on, let's take that boat ride you were talking about." She walked over to the little rowboat, where it sat beached on the bank of the pond. She carefully climbed in. "Hurry up, Earl," she called back. "Get in and push us off." Grandpa meandered over to the boat and hopped aboard. "Quit dawdling and get this boat in the water. I've seen snails that move faster than you," his wife nagged. "Stop your griping," he muttered, reaching for an oar. "We'll get going when I'm good and ready, and not a minute sooner." Positioning the oar against the bank, he pushed off. The boat didn't move. After acquiring a better grip on the oar, he tried again. Still nothing. "Why don't you get out to push off," Grandma suggested. "You can jump back in as soon as the boat is loose." Grandpa reluctantly climbed back out of the boat, braced his foot against a tree, and gave a mighty shove against the bow of the boat. It moved slightly before settling back into place. Gathering his strength, he pushed again. This time, the boat moved half a foot toward the water. "Are you good and ready yet?" Grandma asked him sarcastically. "I'm not getting any younger, you know!" "That's the best news I've heard all day," he snapped back. "At least I can look forward to some peace and quiet!" "What do you mean, peace and quiet?" she asked. "With you being in the shape you are, what could possibly give you the idea that you'll be around after I'm gone?" Grandpa dug in his heels and managed to force the boat nearly into the water. "It really doesn't matter to me which one of us goes first," he declared. "Either way, it means my ears will finally be able to rest!" "Well, I suppose you are entitled to an opinion," Grandma sniffed with a condescending air. "I just want you to realize that, regardless of how you may feel, you most certainly are not in the same shape you were ten years ago. You really do need to slow down." Grandpa made a successful last-ditch effort to launch the boat and then stood there, panting, as it began to bob merrily in tune with the ripples on the pond's glistening surface. "Look at you," Grandma continued. "You're completely out of breath after one simple task. The sweat is dripping off your forehead! I can't hardly imagine how someone in good physical condition could be so worked up after sliding this tiny boat into the water." Grandpa gritted his teeth and took an extremely slow and deep breath. "Wilma," he barked. "Did it ever occur to you that this boat might have been even *slightly* easier to launch without you parked in it? You aren't getting any younger, and you certainly are *not* getting any smaller either!" By this time, the rowboat had drifted slightly out of Grandpa's reach, and Grandma, who felt somewhat offended by his last statement, decided to get to her feet in an attempt to leave the boat. "Steady the boat, Earl," she commanded as she marched to the front. "I won't be wasting any more of my precious day with someone who obviously can't appreciate me for who I am." The sudden movement from within the small boat caused it to sway dangerously. Grandpa made a desperate attempt to reach out and steady it, but missed his target and landed with a loud splash in the shallow water on the edge of the pond! With nothing to keep it upright, the rowboat tipped over, sending Grandma flying into the water, almost onto Grandpa's lap! The two of them sat there in the water for half a minute, glaring at each other. Neither of them could manage even a single word. When they got to their feet, the rowboat was quickly righted and dragged back out of the water. As soon as the boat was safely on the bank, the dishevelled pair stalked over to the four-wheeler and headed back to the house.

Madison was standing by the sink washing dishes while Ben dried and placed them in the cupboard. "I wonder how your grandparents are making out at the pond," Ben remarked. "Hopefully they didn't get the four-wheeler stuck or run into some other trouble." "Don't worry about them too much," Madison answered. "They'll be just fine. Grandma is pretty resourceful, and Grandpa is just too stubborn to let anything slow him down. I'm sure they'll be back at the house any minute, hollering for some breakfast." Ben was setting the last plate in its proper spot, when the distant hum of the returning four-wheeler could be heard. Minutes later, the back door opened and Grandpa and Grandma came trudging in, looking like drowned rats as they dripped all over the floor mat. Grandma immediately removed her soaked footwear and, without a word, stalked downstairs to change. Grandpa did likewise, pausing a moment to offer a brief nod to a stunned Ben and Madison before trailing his wife down the stairs.

"What happened?" asked Ben. "I have no idea, and I'm not sure if I want to know either," commented Madison. "I was going to suggest that you and Grandpa go for a swim in the pool later, but it looks like he beat you to it!"

Charlie

It was Thursday afternoon, and Ben was hard at work. He had just finished his lunch and was eager to get back to business. So far it had been fairly busy, as the weather outside was dark and cloudy with sudden downpours throughout the day. It seemed to Ben that many of the locals who worked outdoors were taking advantage of the dreary weather to get tires rotated and slow leaks fixed. Shortly after lunch, Walter, a framing contractor Ben knew quite well, stopped by after finding that two of the tires on his work truck were flat. "Not sure exactly how I got two flats," Walter grumbled. "I woke up in the morning, and the passenger-side rims were on the ground. I topped both tires up at home with my air compressor, and they stayed full just long enough to get here." "Let's take a quick look," said Ben as he jacked up the side of Walter's truck. Within five minutes, Ben had the two culprit tires off the vehicle and was inspecting the first for leaks.

It didn't take Ben long to find the problem. A nice long nail was embedded in the tire up to its head. He pulled out the spike from the tire, patched the affected area, reseated the tire on its rim, and inflated it. Moving on to the next tire, Ben soon found three more spikes protruding from various locations. He quickly gave the tire the same treatment he had given to the first before balancing and reinstalling them on Walter's truck. Ben showed Walter the four nails he had removed from his tires. "You picked up a few passengers," he chuckled. "Better try not to drop as many nails if you'll be driving on the jobsite." Walter frowned. "I bet it was that kid I hired for summer help," he complained. "He's been with me for half a week, and he already spilled two boxes of nails out of the back of the truck." Ben laughed. "It's not so easy finding good summer help, is it?" he asked. "Tell me about it!" Walter replied. "Don't worry," answered Ben. "It's only been half a week. Maybe he'll get the hang of it soon." "I really hope so," said Walter.

"All right," announced Ben. "Looks like you're good to go." Walter nodded, "Sounds good. What do I owe you?" Ben paused for a moment. Madison's birthday was coming up in a couple of days, and he still had no idea what he was going to get for her. "Didn't your dog just have a litter of puppies?" he asked Walter. "She most certainly did," he replied. "Why, are you in the market for a dog?" "Yeah, I might be. I kind of thought it could be a good birthday present for Madison." Ben said. "Her birthday is this weekend, and I know she's always wanted a nice dog." "Sounds like a good idea," said Walter. "I still have two pups left out of a litter of seven, and it seems like I can't unload this last pair on anyone. I'd keep them myself if I could, but my wife won't let me. She went shopping last week and came home with some real expensive pair of shoes." He stopped to catch his breath. "Who knows what she needed such pricey shoes for anyway," he continued. "But, to make a long story short, she left those new shoes out in the garage, and the two pups had them torn apart in under an hour. I haven't seen her that mad since my chalk line fell off the shelf and spilled red chalk all over the back hall. By the time I noticed, the dog had tracked it all through the kitchen and into the living room!" Ben grimaced. "Sounds like quite the mess." "Oh, believe me," said Walter, "it was. I had to take the dog out back and wash her off with the garden hose." "Well, do you think it would be a fair trade if I take one of your puppies and not bill you for the tires?" asked Ben. "That sounds reasonable," said Walter. "Why don't you stop by my house on the way home once you close up the shop, and you can pick out the one you want?" "Perfect," said Ben. "I should be there just after five."

As five o'clock rolled around, Ben shut down the shop. He locked the front door and pointed his truck in the direction of Walter's house. When he got there, Walter took him into the garage and showed him the two pups. "These ones are almost five months old now, but I'm not sure exactly what kind of dog they are," he explained. "As far as I can tell though, there's a fair bit of border collie in them. They are both male, so you don't have a whole lot of choice in that department." One of the pups came running over to Ben and began to sniff his work boots. Ben picked him up and gave him a once over. "He looks good to me," he told Walter. "Great," Walter replied. "I'll let you borrow a cage to get him home. I can stop by your shop sometime next week to pick it up again." "Sounds good," said Ben, shaking Walter's hand. "I have a feeling that Madison is going to be surprised." Soon they had the dog in a cage and placed him in the back of Ben's truck. Ben thanked Walter, jumped back in the truck, and headed for home.

When he got home, Ben placed the cage containing the puppy next to the back door. Then he went inside to look for Madison. He found her curled up on the couch with a good book and a mug of chamomile tea steaming away on the table beside her. "Hi, honey. How was your day?" he asked her. "Not too bad, I suppose," she replied. "The weather is just so nasty that I felt like staying inside and not moving. I tried to get some lawn mowing done, but the rain didn't let me get very far." "No big deal, there's always tomorrow, I suppose." said Ben. "It looks like the forecast for the rest of the week is pretty clear." "Good," Madison replied. "When we have a day like today I just feel so... blah." Ben smirked. "I know what you mean," he said casually. "But I think I have something that might cheer you up." "Oh really," she answered quickly. "Just what might that be?" "Come with me and find out," said Ben, heading toward the back door. Madison instantly jumped up from the couch and followed him. "What did you get?" she questioned. "Come on, you can tell me." "Wait and see," was Ben's response.

When Ben opened the back door, the puppy was prancing around the small cage, stopping every now and again to let out a high-pitched yelp. Madison was ecstatic. "You got a dog!" she practically shouted. "He's adorable! Where did you find him—it is a him, right?" "Yes," Ben replied, laughing. "It's definitely a him. I got him from Walter. He came into the shop with two flat tires today, and he had a couple of extra puppies from his last litter that he couldn't get rid of. I traded him straight up. Besides," he added, "you have a special day coming up, so I thought I'd surprise you a few days early." Madison looked at him quizzically. "You mean *we* have a special day coming up," she said. Ben stared at her blankly. Madison continued, "You know, our anniversary?" Ben cringed inwardly. How could he have confused her birthday with their anniversary? "Uh, yeah, honey, *we* have a special day coming up. That's what I meant," he backpedaled quickly, trying to fill in the hole that he had started to dig for himself. "Sorry, it was a long day at work." Ben's mind was racing. How could he have been so stupid? Now that he thought about it, he realized that Madison's birthday wasn't for three more months!

That evening over supper, the conversation was centered around the new puppy. "What would be a good name for him?" Madison wondered. "How about Riley," suggested Ben. "I've always liked the sound of that name." "I'm not sure," she mused. "It has to be just the right name." "Maybe Max would be nice," proposed Ben. "He is a boy, so there's no point coming up with some sissy name for him. And he's definitely not the kind of dog that you just stick in your purse and take to the mall to go shopping!" "Of course not," Madison agreed. "Besides, he obviously wouldn't fit in my handbag, and I am not about to go running out to get some big duffel bag for a purse just so I can lug him around all day."

After supper, they took the puppy out of his cage and let him run around the backyard. Ben rummaged about in the hall closet until he found a couple of tennis balls. Taking them outside, he and Madison took turns throwing the balls for the puppy to chase. The small dog seemed to have no trouble finding the brightly coloured tennis balls as they lay in the grass. He charged after each ball as soon as it was thrown, letting out excited yelps of joy while he chased it down. Once the ball came to a stop, he pawed it curiously, batting it around and rolling over top of it on the freshly cut lawn. "He is just *too* cute," Madison gushed as they watched the puppy play. "He seems fairly smart, too," said Ben. "Look, he's bringing the ball back so we can throw it for him again." "We are going to have so much fun with him," Madison stated. "Maybe later this week we could take him for a walk back to the bush and introduce him to the pond." "Yeah, that should be fun," Ben replied.

Later that evening, the puppy had been taken outside for a bathroom trip and given a place in the garage. Ben had put his cage in a corner and nicely arranged an old blanket inside of a cardboard box for him to sleep in. Madison had found some old dishes for his water and food and laid some newspaper down for future use. The lights had been shut off, and the door to the garage closed.

Ben and Madison were upstairs sound asleep. Both were snoring deeply when they were awakened by a piercing howl. Madison dove under the covers, while Ben fumbled for the baseball bat he kept beside the bed. Eventually, they realized the noise was coming from the lonely puppy in the garage. Ben turned on the lamp and glanced at the alarm clock that sat beside him on his nightstand. It was just after three o'clock in the morning. As they sat there wondering what to do, the howling grew louder. "You'd better go and check on the poor little guy," Madison said to Ben. "I guess," he mumbled, rubbing the sleep from his eyes. Ben lurched to his feet and stumbled down the stairs to investigate the racket coming from the garage. When he swung open the door to the garage, he saw the little puppy crouched in the corner of his cage, nose in the air, howling at the top of his lungs. Once the puppy noticed Ben standing in the doorway, he immediately stopped howling and came running over to sniff his feet. "What's the matter, little guy?" Ben asked, reaching down to pet his new friend. The small dog licked his hand and then sat there, wagging his tail and staring at him. Ben went over to inspect the newspaper that Madison had put down for the puppy to use. It was completely dry. He wondered if the puppy wanted to be outside to go to the bathroom. He grabbed a leash from a hook beside the door and gathered the puppy in his arms to take him outside. As soon as they got out of the garage, Ben clipped the leash to the puppy's collar and let him run about. It wasn't long before the excited little pooch had taken care of his business and was ready to go back inside. Placing the puppy back in the garage, Ben flicked off the light and closed the door behind him. He headed back upstairs to bed. When he got there, Madison was already sound asleep. Climbing into bed again, he shut off the lamp and closed his eyes.

In the morning when Ben awoke, everything was quiet. Rolling over, he noticed that Madison had already gotten up. Figuring she must have gone downstairs to take the puppy out for a bathroom trip, he got out of bed and went to find her. Walking out the back door, Ben spotted Madison sitting in a lawn chair, watching the puppy, who was running in circles and chasing his tail. "You know," he said to her. "We really need to name this little fellow." Madison smiled. "Way ahead of you," she said. "His name is Charlie." Ben nodded with a fair degree of satisfaction. "Charlie," he said. "I like the sound of it, but why Charlie?" Madison shrugged her shoulders. "Just because," she answered. "Just because."

Later that morning, Madison was in the kitchen tidying up after a good breakfast. Ben had left for work only a little while earlier, which meant that she was alone with only Charlie for company. "C'mon," she said to him. "Let's go outside and find something to do." On the way out the door, Madison took with her a pair of gardening gloves and a small hoe from inside the back hall closet. She looked around for Charlie, but didn't see him. "Charlie, where are you? Come here, buddy," she called. Charlie came flying around the corner from the kitchen and made a beeline for the open door. He whipped right through Madison's legs in his wild excitement, charging out into the backyard. "Slow down, you goof," Madison called after him as she tugged the door shut behind her. Heading over to the nearest flower garden, she knelt down at the edge and began pulling out weeds while turning over the dark soil. As she worked, she heard a low, growling noise coming from behind her. Casting a glance over her shoulder, she noticed Charlie was picking up the weeds that she had pulled from the ground and discarded. He was vigorously tearing them apart with a passion. Laughing, she continued cleaning out the small garden in front of her, enjoying the bright sunshine. After half an hour of working in the hot sun, Madison was starting to feel quite thirsty. Scooping Charlie under her arm, she went back inside to get some water for herself and the small dog.

Once Madison was back inside the house, she placed Charlie on the floor and started in the direction of the kitchen. Digging around in the cupboards, she found a dish suitable for Charlie and filled it with fresh water from the tap. Madison placed the dish on the floor in front of the puppy and then turned around and headed toward the fridge. Suddenly, her feet flew out from underneath her, and she found herself lying in a clear puddle on the floor. "What in the world?" she muttered under her breath. Madison slowly sat up and tried to collect herself. She dipped her fingers in the puddle and carefully brought them to her nose. As she sniffed, she slowly began to realize that the puddle she was resting in had been deposited there by her new companion, who was thirstily lapping from the dish of water she had placed in front of him. Groaning, Madison got to her feet. She was more than just a little damp. Once she had removed the remainder of the puddle from her kitchen floor, she headed upstairs to change her clothes. When Madison returned to the kitchen, there was another puddle, spread across the linoleum with sparkling perfection, just waiting for her to clean it up. With a deep sigh, she reached for the roll of paper towels.

As the afternoon progressed, the phone rang. When Madison picked it up, Ben was on the other end of the line. "I'm so glad you called," Madison told him. "You'll never guess what happened to me," she said, proceeding to tell him the entire story of how she had wiped out in the kitchen earlier. By the time she was finished telling him what had happened, Ben was gasping for air. "That is awesome," he chortled. "I just wish I could have been there to see it!" "It's not as funny as you think," Madison told him darkly. "You're lucky that you weren't here to see it, or I wouldn't be the only one with a bruise on my rear end." "Oh relax," Ben said. "It's only pee. See you soon. I'll be home in less than an hour." "Okay, love you," she replied, placing the phone back in its cradle. Madison went to the back door to let Charlie in off his leash. Then she lay down on the couch in the living room for a short nap.

It didn't take long for her to fall into a deep sleep. She didn't notice when Ben's truck came crunching down the laneway, and she didn't even stir when he came in through the back door. Madison was still sleeping when he strode into the kitchen and found, with a yelp of surprise, a puddle similar to the ones she had discovered earlier. Even the dull thud of Ben's backside making contact with the kitchen floor failed to rouse her.

Truck Repairs

The morning was warm, with a bright sun shining down. Ben had just come outside after finishing his breakfast. He walked over to his beat-up, old truck. Climbing in, he tossed his lunch pail on the passenger seat and slid the key into the ignition, giving it a slight turn. Click. Ben tried again. Click. He waited for a minute and then gave it another try. Still nothing. He groaned with dismay. Of all the mornings for his truck not to start, this one had to be ranking high on the list for inconvenience. Taking the car was not even an option. Madison had left just ten minutes earlier. She had to start at the daycare before all the parents swarmed in with their carloads of small children. Ben shook his head and thought for a moment. The problem with his truck was probably the start motor, if he went by his past experiences. The truck had run perfectly the day before, although now that he thought about it, the truck had been starting with a greater deal of effort lately. Right now, though, it did not matter to Ben what the problem with the truck was. If he didn't get moving, he would be late to open the shop, something he had always loathed. Heaving a sigh of disbelief, Ben gathered his belongings and climbed back out of the disabled truck. He trudged over to the drive shed, unlocked the door, and slid it open. There parked in front of him was his shiny new four-wheeler. Ben had purchased it only a few short weeks earlier, but to his disappointment, hadn't had much time to ride it yet. In the back of his mind, Ben always knew that the four-wheeler was resting out in the shop, just waiting for him to climb aboard and coax the powerful engine to life. Lately, however, it seemed like something had always come up whenever he felt like going for a ride. Today though, a ride was more of a necessity than a pleasure.

Ben set his lunch pail on the rear rack of the machine and secured it in place with a couple of bungee cords. He walked around to the far side of his new toy and knelt down to check the oil level. Satisfied with what he found, he threw his leg over the seat and turned the key in the ignition. When Ben pressed the green start button, the engine rumbled to life in an instant. He sat there for a minute, enjoying the deep growl of the exhaust. Suddenly, he realized that he was dangerously close to being late for work. He quickly jammed his helmet on his head, tugging the chinstrap to remove the extra slack. Ben pulled out of the drive shed and slid the door shut behind him, clicking the lock securely closed on his way out. He rolled easily down the laneway till he got to the mailbox, and then he punched the throttle, sliding the back end of the machine sideways as he turned onto the gravel road. Loving the rush of adrenaline, Ben straightened out the four-wheeler, keeping his thumb pressed hard on the gas. He sped off toward town, leaving a billowing trail of dust in his wake.

When Ben rode into the parking lot at his shop, he still had a minute or two to spare. Tim had already arrived and had the doors open and the lights on. He had watched Ben pull in on the four-wheeler and was standing behind the front counter with a look of surprise on his face. "What happened to your truck this time?" Tim asked when Ben walked into the shop. "I think it's the start motor," Ben replied, with a cheery smile. "And… this is a good thing?" questioned Tim. Ben grinned. "Well no, not really. But this is the first time in a while that I've been able to go for a decent four-wheeler ride."

At lunchtime, Ben rode over to an auto parts store that was located a few blocks away. It was a place that he frequented whenever something was on the fritz with his truck. Bob, the clerk behind the counter, was ready for him with a big grin on his face when Ben walked in the door. "Hi Ben, do you need another alternator?" Bob laughed, referring to an incident a couple of months earlier. Ben had gone through two alternators in less than a month. He had installed the first alternator, only to have the bearing go a week later. The second had lasted only slightly longer before the same thing happened. Bob had ended up giving him a different alternator at a fraction of the original price to make up for the faulty ones he had received before. Ben grimaced. "I sure hope not. I've seen too many of those things lately." "Don't worry," Bob assured him. "We got rid of that entire product line. It seemed everything we ordered through them was garbage. I guess sometimes that's what happens when you try a new supplier." "Good," said Ben, "because I need a new start motor, and I'd really rather not go through all that hassle again." "No problem," Bob stated. "The line of start motors that I carry is almost bulletproof. I can count on one hand the number of recalls I've had with them over the years." Ben smiled. "Perfect, that's what I need." Bob went to the back and rummaged around for a minute, returning with the appropriate starter for Ben's truck. "That'll be $143.78 with taxes," he said as he scanned the boxed start motor through the cash register. Ben pulled out his wallet and offered his bank card to Bob, who quickly swiped it and handed it back. "Good luck and have a good day," said Bob as Ben stuffed the box under his arm and headed for the door. "Thanks, I'll probably need it," he responded with a grin.

When he returned to Ben's Tire, he found Tim and the rest of his employees run off their feet, trying to keep up to the steady flow of customers. "What happened?" Ben joked, quickly jumping into action. "Did a truck carrying nails flip over on the highway?" Tim managed a weak smile. "You'd almost think so," he replied.

When five o'clock finally rolled around, Ben was more than ready to hit the road. The day had gone by fairly quickly, but the fast pace was still a little tiring. After closing up the shop, he climbed aboard his four-wheeler and booked it for home. The weather was still bright and sunny, and Ben was exhilarated, loving the freedom of flying through the countryside on his new machine. As he rounded the corner into his laneway, Ben knew that he would not let much time pass before his next excursion. He parked the four-wheeler next to his broken-down truck and trotted over to the drive shed to fetch his tools. Madison would not be home for maybe another hour yet, and he wanted to get a good start on swapping out the faulty starter. Ben grabbed his rusty old toolbox from the workbench and carried it over to the truck. "First things first," he told himself. He set the faded toolbox on the gravel laneway beside the truck and made a beeline for the house to find a cold beer. Once inside the house, Ben could hear a faint whining coming from the garage. *Of course!* he thought. Charlie was still shut in the garage where they left him while he and Madison were at work. Ben snatched a beer from the fridge and went to the garage to let out the lonely dog. The instant he opened the door, Charlie was squeezing between his legs and making a mad dash through the kitchen toward the back door. Ben charged after him, intent on letting him out before a small lake appeared on his wife's clean floor. As soon as he was through the door, Charlie was flying in the direction of the nearest tree. He quickly busied himself with the task of relieving the extreme discomfort he had been feeling after being cooped up in the garage nearly all day. Ben popped off the top of the brown bottle that was situated in his right hand and enjoyed a deep swig. He started walking back to the truck to begin removing the old start motor.

Ben positioned his toolbox where he could reach it with a minimal amount of effort and deftly placed his beer beside it. Then he grabbed a couple of wrenches and crawled under the truck in an attempt to catch a glimpse of the faulty starter. Ben quickly spotted the part he needed to remove. He tried the wrenches that were in his hand to see if one of them fit the three bolts that he had to loosen. Ben was surprised to find that the second wrench he tried was the right size. Tossing the other one aside, he firmly positioned the wrench on the head of the bolt and gave it a good yank. It didn't budge. Ben gathered his strength for another try. Taking a deep breath, he pulled with all his might. This time he managed to turn the bolt slightly. Encouraged with the progress he was making, he gave the wrench another turn and soon had the first bolt removed. Ben moved his wrench over to the second bolt and was happy to find that it required even less effort than the first. In no time at all, he had the second bolt out and was focusing his attention on the third. Ben soon realized that the third bolt was not going to be as generous as the previous two had been. No matter how he tugged or pulled, he couldn't seem to move it. Figuring it was a good time to finish his beer, he climbed out from under the truck. As stood there, he tried to think of how he could loosen the last stubborn bolt. Between swallows of smooth lager, Ben decided that he would use the hammer that was lying in the bottom of his toolbox. He figured he could tap the wrench with the hammer and finally loosen the bolt.

Ben finished his beer and dug the hammer out of his toolbox. Then he slipped back under the truck. He slid the wrench onto the seized bolt, and lying on his back, he began to tap it with the hammer. After he had tapped the wrench a few times, Ben felt that it was doing very little to solve his problem. He needed to hit the wrench harder. Winding up, he gave the wrench a solid hit and was immediately rewarded with a shower of rust particles landing on his face. Ben grunted in annoyance and brushed his face clean. It was time to go big or go home, he decided. Shielding his eyes with his spare hand, he mashed his hammer against the wrench with all the force he could muster. The wrench flew off the head of the bolt with good speed, ricocheting off the truck's front tire. It landed on the laneway, about ten feet away. Ben groaned and slid out from underneath the truck to go and find his missing wrench. When he got to his feet, he was just in time to see Charlie scoop up the shiny wrench in his mouth and go tearing across the lawn with it! Ben uttered a deep sigh and began following Charlie around the yard. "Charlie, come," he commanded. Charlie stopped in his tracks and turned to look at him. "Stay there, Charlie," Ben said. The young dog laid the wrench down on the grass in front of him and wagged his tail while he watched Ben approach. "Good boy!" said Ben. He was now within a few feet of the wrench. As he knelt down to pick it up, Charlie growled playfully and snatched the wrench, taking off with it again. As Ben stood there, muttering under his breath, an idea came to him. If he couldn't get close enough to Charlie, maybe Charlie could get close enough to him. Ben turned his back on the energetic puppy and slowly began walking away. Out of the corner of his eye, he could see Charlie beginning to follow him. When he got close, Ben slowed his pace even more, waiting for the dog to get right on his heels. Suddenly, he turned and lunged toward Charlie, shouting out a loud battle cry. To Ben's surprise, he actually managed to capture the puppy before he could take off again. Ben triumphantly reclaimed his prized wrench and set off toward the truck, with the disappointed pooch bringing up the rear.

Before going back under the truck, Ben gave that last bolt a little more thought. He walked over to the drive shed and began rummaging through the pile of scrap metal that lay against the back edge of the building. After a digging around for a while, Ben found a short piece of steel pipe. Taking the pipe with him, he went back to the truck and wormed his way underneath once more. He slid the pipe over the end of the wrench and then applied it to the last bolt. With the extra leverage the pipe provided him, he had no trouble finally breaking the miserable bolt loose. With a cry of glee, Ben removed it from its position and pulled the start motor free. After disconnecting the wiring, he was ready to install the replacement starter.

Once he had wiggled himself out from under the truck, Ben stepped over to the four-wheeler and loosened the bungee cords he had used to hold the new part in place on his journey home. He quickly removed all the packaging from the new start motor and positioned himself, once again, under the truck to begin the process of installing the new part. After he hooked up the wiring, Ben replaced the three bolts in their respective holes and finger tightened them as far as he could manage. He was about to grab the wrench and finish tightening the bolts, when something wet startled him by sliding across the back of his neck. Ben sat straight up, bringing his forehead into contact with the bottom of the truck's frame. Yelping in pain, he rolled over, clutching his forehead in his hands. It didn't take long for the feeling of pain to be replaced with one of anger. Ben scrambled up off the ground and glared at Charlie. Charlie just stared back at him, cocked his head to the side, and barked playfully. Ben couldn't help it.

Standing there, he cracked a smile. "You just wanted to have some fun didn't you, little guy?" he laughed. "Well, I guess that was a pretty good way to get my attention."

As Ben and Charlie stood there staring at each other, Madison's car came rolling down the laneway. When she got out of the car, the first thing Madison noticed were the tools lying around the truck. The second thing she noticed was the large goose egg that was forming on Ben's forehead. "What in the world have you two been up to?" she asked suspiciously, glancing around. "Oh, nothing much," answered Ben. "What's for supper?" Madison gave him a dirty look. "How about a bag of ice for your forehead." she stated. "Sounds good to me, honey," Ben replied. "Lead the way."

Over a supper of grilled cheese and fresh garden salad, Ben filled Madison in on the details of his day, beginning with his early morning four-wheeler ride and ending with how he had developed the large, discoloured egg on his forehead. "Wow," she mentioned, when he was done with his story. "You had an interesting day, and it sounds like Charlie was keeping you entertained." "Yeah, I suppose he was," Ben responded. "But the good news is, I only have to tighten the bolts holding the starter in place, and then I'm all finished." Madison smiled, "Great, then we can take the truck when you come with me to do groceries like you promised last week." Ben stared blankly across the table at her before it dawned on him. Maybe he had promised something along those lines the week before. When they were done eating, he closed the meal with prayer and quickly went back outside to the truck to finish torquing the three bolts. Charlie had seemingly lost interest in the happenings near the truck and was lying on the sidewalk, resting. With Charlie out of the way Ben was able to complete his task without interruption. After he was done with the bolts, Ben opened the driver's door of the truck and turned the key. The truck instantly rumbled to life, giving him the satisfying feeling of a job well done. Ben shut off the truck and began cleaning up his various tools. He had just parked the four-wheeler in the drive shed when Madison called out the window that she was ready to go. "Be there in a minute," he replied. "Hurry up," she said, "You're filthy dirty from lying under that old truck. Get in here and take a quick shower before we go."

Once Ben had gotten himself more or less presentable, he and Madison put Charlie in the garage and left for town. When they arrived at the grocery store, Ben swung the truck into the first available parking space and shut off the engine. "I'll get a cart," he told Madison, as he dashed off toward the corral where the carts were kept. A few minutes later, they were cruising up and down the aisles of the store, doing their best to find everything on the list that Madison had hastily scrawled out before they left home. Soon the cart was almost full, and they had managed to check off most of the items on the list. They slowly made their way to the checkout at the front of the store. Once the girl working the checkout had scanned everything through, Madison pulled out her wallet to pay, while Ben started loading everything back into the cart. Madison collected the receipt, and she and Ben headed for the exit.

Soon the old truck was following their familiar path back home. Ben was behind the wheel, describing with great pride to Madison the amount of money he had saved that day by replacing the worn-out start motor himself. "If we had taken the truck to a mechanic, we would have been charged a fortune," he told her. "That's great, honey," she told him. "I know," he replied. "And the best part is that it was such a simple repair. I knew exactly what I was doing." Madison reached over and switched on the radio. Instantly, the truck was filled with the sounds of her favourite station. She leaned back in her seat, enjoying the music. As they listened, they noticed that the speakers were beginning to crackle. Suddenly, the radio just quit. Ben and Madison glanced at each other. "That doesn't make sense," Ben scowled. "I just put that radio in here a little while back." Then the dashboard went dim, and the truck itself quit running. Ben's scowl got darker. He pulled the truck onto the shoulder of the road and got out to open the hood. When he did, it took a minute for the smoke to clear. Looking around more closely, he noticed that one of the cables running to the battery was almost bare. In fact, the insulation that should have covered the copper wire was melting and dripping off. Ben stuck his head under the truck and groaned inwardly. Earlier, in his hurry to install the new starter, he hadn't noticed that the cable feeding the starter was resting snugly against the hot exhaust pipe. Madison rolled down her window to ask him a simple question. "Will the money you saved by fixing it yourself be enough to cover a tow truck?"

Yard Work

Running along the side of the laneway was a cedar hedge. The hedge was changing colour. It had been there for years, long before Ben and Madison had moved into the house, and for reasons unknown, it was dying. One evening, over supper, Madison had mentioned to Ben that the hedge was starting to look shabby and rundown. Ben had nodded absentmindedly and mumbled something about taking a look at the hedge when he had a spare moment. As time passed, it seemed clear to Madison that Ben wasn't very interested in finding a spare moment, a moment which he could spend devising a plan on how to deal with the hedge. The hedge continued to change appearance, from a deep green to a ratty-looking brown. Ben suggested that perhaps it was merely starting to change colour in the fall, with the rest of the trees. Madison had stared at him scornfully before sarcastically asking if he understood the term "evergreen." It was then that Ben realized she expected him to do something about the disintegrating hedge. So it came to pass that, bright and early the next Saturday morning, Ben was standing next to the hedge, revving out a chainsaw, with a look of malicious intent written across his features.

Ben attacked the hedge with vigour. He ran the chainsaw along the lower half of the cedars, leaving stumps that were roughly a foot high. He supposed that it would be a fairly simple task to wrap a nylon strap around the stumps later and pull each one out with his four-wheeler. By the time he reached the halfway point of the laneway, Ben was breathing hard. The morning had already turned fairly warm, and the sweat was beginning to drip from his brow. Ben grasped the bottom hem of his T-shirt and pulled it up over his head, using it to wipe the beads of sweat off his forehead. The warm breeze felt great on his hot skin. Ben decided that now would be a good time to check the fluids in the chainsaw. He unscrewed the cap from fuel reservoir and noticed that it was nearly dry. Picking up the chainsaw, he carried it over to the drive shed to look for some mixed fuel. Finding none, he began to look around for some two-stroke oil to mix with gas.

After rooting through the various cupboards and drawers, Ben was convinced that he had used the last of the oil. He was about to go find his truck keys so he could buy some oil when he saw the weed trimmer hanging beside the shed door. The trimmer, Ben remembered, ran on the same mix as the chainsaw. *Maybe there was still some fuel in the tank*, he thought. Wandering over to the trimmer, he took it off its hook and inspected it for leftover fuel. "Yes!" said Ben out loud. The trimmer had nearly a full tank of fuel in it. Hopefully that would be enough to serve his purpose of cutting down the hedge. Ben quickly transferred the fuel from the trimmer into the saw. Then he topped off the bar oil from a container sitting on the workbench. He left the chainsaw resting there on the bench and headed to the house in search of something to drink.

When he got to the house, he found Madison sitting at the kitchen table going over some bills. Ben groped around in the fridge until he located the brown bottle he had been searching for. Watching Madison closely, he twisted off the cap and took a deep swig. As soon as she heard the noise of the cap coming off the bottle in Ben's hand, Madison looked up at him in disbelief. "It's only 10:30 in the morning," she protested. "Why are you drinking beer already?" She received a smug smile in return. "I was up pretty early," Ben stated. "And I've been working hard. I think I could do with a cold beer, don't you?" Madison shrugged her shoulders. "I suppose one beer couldn't hurt. It just seems a little early, that's all. How's it going with the hedge out there? I haven't heard the chainsaw in a while, are you done?" Ben grinned. "Don't worry about it," he said. "I've got about half of it cut down, and I'm almost ready to turf the rest." He drained the remnants of his beer and set the empty bottle on the counter next to the sink. "Well, good luck," said Madison as he headed back outside.

Ben stopped by the drive shed to grab the chainsaw, which he had left on the workbench. Whistling, he continued on his way to the hedge he had been dismantling. Giving the pull cord a sharp yank, Ben brought the chainsaw to life. He gave the trigger a good squeeze and resumed work where he had left off earlier. Soon there was a long row of decapitated cedars strung out along the length of the gravel laneway. Ben was closing in on the end of the hedge when the saw began to sputter. "C'mon baby," he muttered, quickening his pace. He turned the small machine on its side in an attempt to coax every possible drop of fuel from the tank. Of the bushes that earlier in the morning had resembled a hedge, only one remained. Ben was scrambling to finish the row before he ran out of fuel. He jabbed the chainsaw toward the base of the little cedar and was almost through when the saw choked to a halt and the chain stopped turning. Ben was somewhat disappointed. He had come so close only to miss by such a small amount. "Oh well," he told himself. "Close enough." Looking back along the edge of the laneway, Ben took a small measure of satisfaction in the mess that lay on the ground where the hedge had once stood. Wiping away the sweat that was running down his forehead, he toted the chainsaw over to the drive shed to exchange it for a shovel.

Ben trudged around the drive shed, trying to find his shovel. He couldn't remember the last time he had used it, and he definitely did not remember where he had left it. As he searched around the shed, he spotted his axe leaning against the wall. Figuring it would come in handy for cutting through the gnarled roots that were holding the stumps in place, Ben grabbed it and kept looking for the shovel. Finally he found it, hiding in the corner behind a pile of old tarps. Taking his newly compiled arsenal with him, he hurried back to the line of stumps that bordered the laneway. Ben slid the shovel deep into the rich soil that covered the first stump. He worked his way around it, exposing the mess of roots. By the time he had ten of the stumps uncovered, Ben was feeling a bit winded. Opting for an easier task, he walked away, returning a few minutes later with the four-wheeler and a nylon strap. Ben backed the machine up to the row of stumps. Taking the nylon strap, he wrapped one end around the closest stump and secured the other end to the back of the four-wheeler. Ben jumped back on the machine and idled ahead until most of the slack in the strap was gone. Then he punched the throttle, giving the stump a good jerk. The stump came halfway out of the ground and then settled back into place. Ben reversed the four-wheeler and tried again. This time, the stump jumped out of the ground, leaving a fair sized hole behind it. Ben lost no time in moving the strap to the next stump and pulling again. After a couple attempts, the second stump was lying beside the first, with its roots exposed to the withering sun. Ben kept moving, and soon the pile of evicted cedar stumps began to grow. Looping the strap over the next stump, he climbed aboard the four-wheeler and hit the gas. The four-wheeler bogged down from the load and then sprang ahead as the strap slipped off the stump and flew through the air. The strap hit Ben squarely on his bare, sweaty back. He doubled over, clenching his teeth in pain. Kneeling on the ground beside the four-wheeler, he breathed heavily and rubbed his sore back. After he got back to his feet, he decided on a new course of action. He parked the four-wheeler off to the side and went to the house to find his truck keys.

Ben marched into the kitchen, hot and sweaty. Digging his truck keys out of a container on the counter, he stuffed them into his pocket. Then he found a tall glass in the cupboard and filled it with fresh water from the tap. Madison was gathering together the papers she had been working with that had been strewn across the kitchen table. "I just finished with these bills," she announced. "How are you making out with the hedge?" Ben turned around to show her the raised welt on his back. By this time, it had turned a bright, fire engine red. Madison looked at the welt with horror. "What are you doing out there, trying to get hurt?" she asked. Ben took a swallow of cool water. "It's no big deal," he said. "I was pulling out a stump with the four-wheeler, and the strap I was using slipped off." Madison looked at him sympathetically. "Why don't you use the truck to pull out the stumps?" she suggested. "Then you can't get hurt." Ben dug the truck keys out of his pocket and dangled them in front of her. "Way ahead of you, honey," he stated. Madison smiled. "Just be careful," she said.

Ben backed the truck up to the row of stumps. Once again, he wrapped the nylon strap around one of them. Then he looped the opposite end over the truck's ball hitch. He threw the truck into four-wheel low and pressed down on the accelerator. The truck rolled forward so easily that Ben assumed the strap had slipped off again. When he walked around to the back of the truck to check on the strap, he was surprised to find the stump still securely attached. Ben stood there for a moment, surveying the remaining stumps. He had pulled out all the ones he had dug around, but if the truck had pulled out the last one so easily, maybe he didn't need to do anymore digging. Ben decided the idea had merit. The less digging the better, he supposed. He hooked up to another stump and was impressed with how little effort it took to remove it. Impressed with his success, Ben figured he would try to pull two stumps at a time. He ran the strap around two that were close together and got back in the truck. The truck offered no complaint, and soon, the two cropped cedars were on the growing pile with all the rest. Ben kept moving at a steady pace, pulling multiple stumps at a time. Soon he was at the end of the row, with only the last stubborn cedar left, the one he had been unable to finish cutting earlier. Ben parked the truck at the end of the row, got out, and stared at the defiant piece of greenery. It stood there, rooted in place, with no plans to leave. Ben wondered if it was taunting him. He paced around the small cedar that he supposed would be his next victim, pausing to spit at its base. He hooked it up to the truck and got back in the cab. With a feeling of anticipation, Ben revved the engine a few times before he put the truck in gear. He tromped on the gas pedal and the truck surged ahead. Ben felt a sharp tug on his hitch and a split second later, heard the sound of shattering glass. Glancing over at the seat on his right, Ben was shocked to see that the cedar he meant to pull from the ground had gone a step further and become a passenger in his vehicle. He stopped the truck, killed the engine, and got out to take a look. Though it seemed obvious to Ben what had happened, he still wasn't ready to accept it. *Why was he so stupid*, he wondered? *Why had he gotten so carried away?* As Ben stood there, miserably staring at the damage, he saw Madison walking over from the house. Charlie was loping along behind her. Ben knew he was going to hear it from Madison. He contemplated pretending he hadn't seen her, jumping back in the truck, and leaving to get the window fixed before she could ever find out. It seemed like a good plan. He could get the window fixed, hide the bill, and no one would be the wiser. As Ben grasped the door handle to get into the truck, he stole a glance at Madison as she approached. The look on her face told Ben that she was onto him and escape would be useless. "What did you do?" Madison shouted. She had already seen the shattered window, but when she caught a glimpse of the mangled cedar lying in the front seat, her eyes grew large. Ben stared at the ground, trying to think of some way he could make the situation seem more trivial. He could think of nothing. "Well, honey," he replied. "The sun was in my eyes." Madison stood there, staring him down. "What kind of a dumb excuse is that?" she demanded. Ben was silent. She continued, "I just came out to tell you that lunch is ready, so hurry up and get in the house before it gets cold." Madison turned on her heel and stalked back to the house, with Ben following behind her meekly. Charlie, sensing the tension, had wisely decided to make himself scarce.

Over lunch, Madison seemed to calm down significantly. Ben had finally gathered the courage to explain to her what had happened. "It's really no big deal, honey," he said. "A new window can't be more than a few hundred bucks. I saved a lot more than that by taking out those trees myself." Madison glared at him. "It's not about how much money you saved. You could have been really hurt." Ben grinned. "But I wasn't," he pointed out. "So it really doesn't matter." Madison scowled. "Just be more careful," she said.

After lunch, Madison took the truck into town to get a new window put in. When she had left, Ben hooked up his little trailer to the four-wheeler and began bringing loads of the dismembered hedge to the burn pit behind the house. It took several trips, but eventually Ben had everything ready to burn. With that task completed, he drove the trailer to the pile of topsoil they kept next to the drive shed. He filled the trailer until the tires began to bulge and the soil was ready to spill out. Then he carefully drove to the edge of the laneway and began filling in the holes that the hedge had left behind. As he was working away, Ben heard a faint growling noise coming from the other side of the yard. Turning, he saw Charlie fighting with a piece of the cedar hedge he had stolen off of the burn pile. Ben sighed. He marched over to the dog and sternly rebuked him. Afterward, he brought the stolen item back to the pile for burning. Returning to work, Ben managed to finish filling the holes in record time. When he looked up, there was Charlie, dragging another branch across the yard. This time, Ben was a little frustrated. He pulled the branch away from Charlie and returned it to the burn pit. Now he went to the drive shed and got a jerry can filled with gasoline. Ben poured the gas over the pile of brush and struck a match and threw it on. The pile was blazing in no time. Ben brought the garden hose over just in case the fire got out of hand. Then he stood there with a watchful eye.

Madison was on her way home from town. Surprisingly, Ben had been accurate with his guess of how much the replacement window would cost. When she turned onto their road, Madison could see the smoke from the fire rising into the air. She was about to turn into the laneway when she did a double take. There was Charlie, tearing across the yard with what appeared to be a burning branch grasped firmly in his teeth. Ben was chasing after him with the garden hose in hand. Madison just shook her head and kept driving.

Rain and a Roof

It was a rainy Friday afternoon. Madison stood at their bedroom window, looking out over the backyard. The rain was pounding on the roof, with the wind howling against the brick walls of the house. Madison could hardly believe the amount of rain they had received over the course of the day. The laneway resembled a series of miniature lakes, as the potholes were all overflowing with water. As she searched around the backyard with her blue eyes, Madison noticed that the shingles on the small garden shed in the corner of the yard were beginning to break off in the high winds. She kept glancing at the little building, wondering if its roof could withstand the elements until the storm had run its course. While Madison was keeping watch on the garden shed, she saw some more shingles tear away from the roof and fly through the air to land in the swimming pool. She frowned. Something had to be done. Madison went downstairs to the kitchen to pour herself a mug of coffee. While she was sipping the warm drink, an idea came to her. She would go to the hardware store and buy the shingles that were needed. Then tomorrow morning, while Ben was working, she would replace the failing roof herself. Madison had never done any roofing before, but the more she thought about it, the more she became attached to the idea. It was, after all, such a small roof. How hard could it be? Madison quickly finished the last of her coffee. She put on her coat, grabbed an umbrella from the closet, and dashed out into the downpour to the car.

Madison pulled up in front of the hardware store and scrambled out of her car. She raced across the sidewalk into the store, trying to dodge the raindrops along the way. The door eased closed behind her. An older man with grey hair, who was standing behind the counter, looked up from the computer he had been tapping away at. "What can I do for you?" he asked pleasantly. Madison read his name tag and smiled. "Well, Andrew, I need some shingles," she announced, adding proudly, "I'm re-shingling my garden shed." Andrew grinned. "At least you seem excited," he commented. "What type of shingle were you looking for?" Madison had to think for a minute. Right now the shed was grey with a grey roof to match, but it had never occurred to her that she might change the colour of the roof. "Brown," she said, suddenly. "I'll take some brown shingles, just something plain." The roof of their house was brown, and Madison decided it might look nice to coordinate the two. Andrew produced a sheet from behind the counter with various colour samples of shingles attached to it. "Which shade of brown?" he asked. Madison studied the sheet for a few moments before pointing to the one she wanted. "Okay," said Andrew. "How many bundles do you need?" Madison gazed back at him with a blank expression on her face. 'Um… I'm not exactly sure," she mumbled sheepishly. Andrew just laughed. "I'll tell you what. You go to the back of the store and stick your head out the door. You'll see three different garden sheds sitting in the corner of the yard. Take a look, then come back and let me know which one is the closest in size to yours." Madison breathed a sigh of relief. "I'll be right back," she said, trotting off to catch a glimpse of the sheds. Once Madison got to the back door of the store, she stuck her head out and took a peek at the three garden sheds. The first two were definitely much smaller than the one she had at home, but the third seemed fairly close to the same size. Madison walked back to the counter at the front of the store. "I think the biggest shed you have there is almost the same size," she told Andrew. He looked up from his computer again. "Okay, good. Now you said almost the same size. Is your shed bigger or smaller?" "A bit bigger, I think." she replied. Andrew nodded thoughtfully. "All right," he said. "I'll give you enough shingles for the bigger shed I have out there, and I'll give you a couple of extra bundles for good measure. If you still end up running short, you know where to find me, and I've got lots more so don't worry." Madison smiled cheerfully. "That sounds like it should work. How much will the bill come to?" "That depends," Andrew replied. "What quality of shingle do you want? I've got shingles that will last anywhere from fifteen to forty years." Madison said, "I'll take whatever's cheapest. It's just a shed, after all." Andrew began tapping away on his computer and quickly came up with a price for the shingles. "Will you be needing any nails?" he asked. "No, thank you, I've got lots," Madison answered, remembering the bags of nails that had been strewn all over Ben's workbench the last time she had been in the drive shed. "Then you're all set," declared Andrew, printing out a receipt from his computer. "Give the white copy to the cashier, and keep the pink copy for the guys in the yard. Just pull your vehicle around back and they'll load you up."

When Madison left the hardware store, the back of her small car was riding considerably lower than the front. In fact, if you didn't know any better, you might be tempted to think that the front wheels of the car would lift off the ground at any given moment. The guys who worked in the yard at the store had just barely been able to fit the last bundle of shingles into her trunk. If she had looked in her rearview mirror as she pulled out of the yard, she would have seen them standing there with smirks on their faces, staring at the rear of her car as she disappeared around the corner.

By the time she was home again, the rain had stopped. Madison parked the car beside the drive shed and popped the trunk. Next, she opened the shed, fired up the four-wheeler, and brought it out beside the car so she could load the shingles onto it. Soon, she had all the bundles out of the trunk and lying across the four-wheeler on the racks. Madison reversed the machine back into the drive shed and shut it off. She wandered around Ben's workbench for a few minutes, searching for the nails she would need tomorrow. As she examined the contents of the many brown paper bags that were covering the bench, she quickly came up with what she assumed would be a reasonable quantity of nails to work with. Madison set the nails she had collected on the shingles that covered the four-wheeler. She was about to walk away when she noticed that each bundle of shingles came with detailed instructions printed on the plastic packaging. As she scanned the instructions for details on what to do tomorrow, her confidence began to build. From what she was reading, shingling a roof didn't seem all that complicated. Madison was excited. She had watched her dad replace old roofs before, and she remembered how easy he had made it seem. While she was reminiscing, she also seemed to remember, rather clearly, the task of picking up all the old nails and pieces of shingles after the original roof had been torn off. She had hated that chore, but it had always been she who was given the responsibility of carrying it out. Her dad had always told her that he wanted her to do it, because he knew she was the only one, out of her siblings, who would do a proper job. The more Madison thought about that miserable task, the less she wanted to do it again. Finally, she decided that she would just install the new shingles right over top of the old ones. Standing there in the drive shed, she suddenly realized that she would need, at the very least, a hammer to pound in the nails. She looked around the building, hoping to spot what she needed. After searching for a few minutes, the closest thing she could find was the sledgehammer that was next to the door. Madison wracked her brain, trying to think of where Ben would have left his hammer and tool apron. She began rooting through the various drawers and cupboards in an attempt to locate the missing items. Eventually, she found the hammer attached to Ben's apron. It was stuffed in the deepest corner on the bottom shelf of an old cabinet. She carried both items over to the four-wheeler and placed them beside the bags of nails. Just then Madison heard Ben pull into the laneway, coming home from work. She quickly left the drive shed, sliding the door shut on her way out so he wouldn't see the pile of shingles. She ran over to meet him.

Ben had picked up burgers and fries for supper on his way home from work. The sun was out now, and the temperature had risen drastically. "Come on, honey," he said to Madison. "Let's eat outside on the patio." Soon they were sitting outside on the lawn furniture, a drink in one hand and a burger in the other, enjoying the sudden heat wave at the end of a wet, dreary day. Charlie lay under the table in the shade, panting from the unexpected heat, just waiting for a scrap of food to fall on the ground in front of him. Once their meal was finished, they just sat there, soaking up rays from the setting sun and talking about each other's day. Eventually Ben got tired of sitting. "Let's go for a walk," he said. Madison smiled. "That would be kind of nice," she replied. "Why don't we take Charlie with us?" Ben nodded. "Sure, that should be fun," he said rising from his chair. "I'll get his leash."

As they walked down the gravel road, enjoying the countryside, a large jackrabbit bounded across the road just in front of them. Charlie lunged forward, straining at his leash, yelping excitedly. Madison chuckled at the small dog's antics. "Easy, boy," Ben told him. "You'll never catch that guy; he's way too fast for you." They continued walking from tree to tree, appreciating the shade each one cast that protected them from the stifling heat. Five minutes later, Madison turned to Ben and suggested that they turn around and go for a swim to cool down instead. Ben was more than happy to agree, so they reversed their path and headed for the pool. As soon as they got to the end of the laneway, Ben dropped the leash, and he and Charlie sprinted for the pool at top speed. Reaching the edge, Ben never slowed down but jumped right into the cool, sparkling water. Charlie jumped and yelped, running circles around the pool, wanting to be in with Ben. Shortly after, Madison kicked off her shoes and dove into the pool to join him. They splashed and fought in the refreshing water until they were tired. Then they just lay there, floating and feeling revitalized. While they were lounging around the pool, Ben noticed some pieces of shingles lying on the bottom. "I'm going to have to do something about that shed roof," he stated. "It's starting to become a problem." Madison rubbed his shoulders. "Don't worry, dear," she told him. "There's no rush."

The next morning, Ben was up bright and early and left for work. No sooner was his truck gone in a trail of dust then Madison was out the back door, wearing old clothes and ready to do some roofing. She made a beeline for the drive shed, dodging Charlie as he ran underfoot. Madison slid open the shed door and marched over to the four-wheeler. She jumped aboard and cranked the engine to life. She carefully idled out onto the laneway and across the backyard toward the garden shed. Madison parked the four-wheeler in front of the little shed and dismounted. Nearby was a small wooden picnic table. She dragged it over to the wall of the shed and climbed on top. The small table made a perfect platform from which she could work. Standing on top, Madison could just reach the peak of the roof. She grabbed a bundle of shingles and some nails from the four-wheeler, strapped on Ben's tool apron and hammer, and got back up on the picnic table. Madison studied the instructions on the package once more and slowly began her first row of shingles.

Once the starter strip was complete, she started running the shingles across in a careful fashion. She lined up the tabs on each side and cut off whatever excess was left when she reached the other end of the roof. Madison brought over a few more bundles of shingles and began to pick up the pace. Soon she was almost at the peak of the shed. She reached down for her next shingle and was surprised to find nothing there. Madison had been sure that another shingle was lying on the table. Out of the corner of her eye, she saw Charlie ripping around the yard, dragging something behind him. Turning around, she soon realized that it was the missing shingle in his mouth. Madison shook her head and climbed down from the table to get her next bundle. "At least he'll be out of way," she muttered. Using the bundle of shingles she had just grabbed, Madison was able to reach the peak of the roof. She glanced over at the remaining bundles on the four-wheeler. As near as she could figure, without actually counting, she had already used just about half of the pile of shingles that were weighing down the four-wheeler. Madison took a deep breath, hoping that she would have enough to finish. Then she went inside to get a drink and to find out what time it was.

The clock in the kitchen told her that she had less than three hours before lunch and the end of Ben's workday. Madison threw back a tall glass of water and hurried back to the shed to start the other side of the roof. Right away, she moved the table she had been working from to the opposite side of the small building. She loaded it with the remaining shingles, setting the four-wheeler free from the extra weight it had been supporting. Madison began with the starter strip once again and settled into a rhythmic pace, laying a shingle on the roof and fastening it down with a few nails. One nail on each end of the shingle and then two more nails in the middle. She was making good time hammering away. Meanwhile, Charlie lay at the base of the table, staring at his captured shingle. In what seemed to her like a short amount of time, Madison was at the peak of the roof again. She pulled Ben's knife out of his apron and began cutting the remaining shingles into caps to place along the ridgeline of the roof. When she was done cutting, Madison started at one end, fastening the caps to the roof. By the time she was halfway across, she realized she would be very close to having the right amount of shingles. Madison kept up the pace, knowing she was nearing the end of the job. When she reached the far side of the roof, she found that she was only two caps short. She stood there disappointed, wishing she could find just one more shingle so she could finish. Then she saw Charlie lying on the ground with his stolen shingle in front of him. "Charlie, stay," she commanded. Charlie immediately picked up the shingle and started to run away. Madison quickly dove on top of him, rescuing the badgered shingle from his grasp. One end of the shingle was nearly torn apart, but the other two tabs seemed fairly usable. Within a couple minutes, she had the shingle cut into caps and fastened to the roof. She climbed down from the picnic table and stood back a few feet to survey her handiwork. Madison had to admit to herself that she was a bit surprised. The roof actually looked quite good. She slid the picnic table back to its original place and started gathering all the leftover plastic packaging. Madison went to the house and got a black garbage bag. She put all the plastic scraps in it and placed it in the trash can beside the garage. Then she parked the four-wheeler in the drive shed and put Ben's hammer and apron back where she had found them. Madison glanced at the roof of the garden shed as she walked back to the house. The more she looked at it, the better it seemed. She was quite proud of herself. In less than half a day, she had transformed the old, leaky roof into something that not only looked good but would last for what she hoped would be years to come.

When Ben got home from work, Madison lost no time in pointing out to him the new roof on the garden shed. "Wow, honey," he exclaimed. "You did that all by yourself?" Madison nodded modestly. "With a little help from Charlie," she said. Ben walked over to the shed to take a better look. "Wow," he said again. "It looks really good. I didn't know you knew how to shingle." "Neither did I," Madison replied. Ben opened the shed door and ducked inside. As soon as he stood up, he let out a yelp of pain. He stumbled back out of the shed, rubbing his head gingerly. "What's the matter?" Madison asked him. "I got poked in the top of the head with a nail," he told her. "How long were the nails you used?" Madison stared at him. "I'm not sure," she answered. "I just grabbed some of the nails that were lying on your workbench in the drive shed." Ben laughed. "No wonder I can't stand up in there anymore," he chuckled. "Those nails are about two inches longer than you needed, and I could hardly stand up in there before." Madison glared at him. "I tried to do something nice for you, and you just laugh at me," she said accusingly. "How was I supposed to know not to use those nails?" Ben was still laughing. "Don't worry, honey," he told her. "I'll just learn to duck."

A Car Ride

The alarm clock sounded with a piercing racket, rousing Ben and Madison from the restful sleep they had been busying themselves with. Sunlight was beginning to peek through the cracks of the blinds that hung in front of their bedroom window, signalling that day was about to begin. Madison tucked her head under her pillow. She jammed it tightly against her ears, trying to drown out the incessant beeping that the alarm clock was producing. Ben grunted and rolled over, still half asleep. They both lay there for a moment, pretending that the morning had not yet arrived. Eventually, the alarm clock quieted, going into snooze mode, and leaving the bedroom almost silent. Only the sound of Ben's rhythmic snoring was left to break the tranquility. Five minutes later, they were still lying there, mostly asleep. The alarm clock sprang to life once again, with an intensified energy. Ben just lay there, sprawled across the bed in a sleep-induced coma. He finally woke up after receiving a sharp elbow in the ribs from his irritated wife. "Honey," she moaned groggily, "do something with that stupid clock!" Ben rolled over again and began slapping the nightstand beside the bed in a half-hearted attempt to end the noise. Within seconds, he received another elbow in the ribs. This one was more vicious than the first, firmly encouraging him to get serious about dealing with the alarm clock. He opened one eye and spotted the clock, sitting on the edge of the nightstand. Ben reached out and took a clumsy swing at the small clock, knocking it off the nightstand and onto the bedroom floor, where it continued to shriek at them. By the time he was given a third elbow, Ben was fairly certain that he was going to have a nice bruise. He threw his legs over the side of the bed, got up, and stumbled across the room in a blurry stupor, looking for the displaced alarm clock. Soon he found it, managed to turn it off, and replaced it on the nightstand. Madison finally removed the pillow that had been protecting her ears from the alarm clock's penetrating din. She sat up in bed and glanced across the room at Ben. "We'd better get moving," she remarked. "We promised my parents we'd be at their place shortly after lunch." He stared back at her with a blank expression. "That's today?" he mumbled. "Yes, Ben. Today. I told you we're going there for the long weekend, remember?" Madison asked. "It's been written on the calendar for weeks. My mom keeps phoning to remind us, and I even told you again at supper last night." Ben sighed. Her parents lived almost four hours north of them. It wasn't that he didn't want to visit. He just knew he was going to hate being stuck in the car for hours on end as they cruised along the highway. Whenever Ben and Madison went on a long drive, there were only two possible scenarios. Either Ben was behind the wheel, booking it in the passing lane, with Madison sitting beside him, telling him to watch the road and slow down. Or she was driving and Ben was in the passenger seat, bored out of his mind, wishing for the trip to be over. Right now, either course of action was entirely unappealing to him. "I guess we'd better start packing," he muttered slowly. "Way ahead of you," Madison announced. "You're always really slow in the morning, so I packed a bag for each of us yesterday while you were at work." Ben nodded. "I suppose that makes this kind of easy then, doesn't it?" Madison shot him a smug grin. "That was the plan, genius. I topped off the car and we can stop on the way for a buffet breakfast at that truck stop you like." Ben rubbed his belly fondly, anticipating a delicious meal of bacon, sausage, eggs, and french toast. "Don't just stand there," Madison told him. "Get some clothes on and go dig your fishing rod out of the garage. I promised my dad you would go fishing with him tomorrow morning. You know how he loves to go fishing every Saturday."

Less than an hour passed before they were pulling out of the laneway, bags and fishing rod in the trunk. Charlie lay on an old blanket in the back of the car, panting with the excitement of going for a ride. "Hang on, boy," Ben told him. "It's just for a little while. Then Tim will look after you." Minutes later, they were on Tim's front step, ringing the doorbell. Ben could hear some muffled noises coming from inside the house. He suspected it was Tim, making his way down the hall to the door. An instant later, the door swung open, proving Ben's suspicions correct and displaying a groggy Tim. He was clad in wrinkled pyjamas and munching on what appeared to be a bagel. "Morning, bro," Tim greeted him. "Man, you guys are early. You want a bagel or something?" Ben glanced at the sorry-looking breakfast that Tim was clutching in his left hand and shook his head. "No, thanks. We're going to take a break at the truck stop for a bite to eat on our way up north." Tim shrugged his shoulders. "Have it your way," he said. "Where's Charlie?" Ben looked over his shoulder. "Madison's getting him out of the car. I hope you're well rested, he'll probably be pretty hyper." Tim grinned. "Perfect. I was just about to go jogging."

Ben was flying along in the fast lane with the cruise control set and the radio tuned to his favourite station. He switched lanes a few times to manoeuvre around a couple of slower vehicles. He cast a glance toward Madison. "We should be stopping to eat breakfast in ten or fifteen minutes," he commented. "How's your appetite?" Madison grimaced and reached into the backseat for a magazine to bury her nose in. "It would be better if you weren't weaving through traffic like a maniac," she replied. "If you're going to drive like this the entire way, then I'd rather take over after we eat." Ben smiled. "Feel free," he stated. "You're more than welcome."

Half an hour later, Madison was sitting in a padded booth in the truck stop. She was sipping a steaming mug of coffee and staring across the table at her husband, who was hastily devouring plate after plate of delicious food. "Don't overdo it like the last time we were here," she warned him. "We've still got a long drive ahead of us." "Hey," said Ben, taking time out to glance up from the food on the table in front of him. "How often do I get to come here and enjoy a good all-you-can-eat breakfast?" Madison smiled at him. "Not often," she admitted. "But I don't want to hear you whining about a sore stomach and how bloated you feel for the rest of the trip." Ben shot her an amused look. "Don't worry. When I'm done eating, I'll hit the restroom, and I'll be good to go for the rest of the drive."

When they were finished with their meal, Madison went up to the cashier to pay, while Ben gingerly extracted himself from the booth and tottered over to the restroom to relieve some internal pressure. In no time at all, they were in the car again and merging back onto the highway. "Thanks for offering to drive, honey," mentioned Ben from the passenger seat where he was sprawled. His arms were folded across his stuffed belly and a contented smile was spread over his face. "Believe me," Madison answered, "it's my pleasure."

As they drove along, Ben drifted off to sleep and began to snore rather loudly. Madison cranked up the radio a little, trying to cover up his wheezing. She began to hum along to the song that was playing. As she hummed, she smoothly piloted the car through the early morning traffic. They were making good time as they headed toward her parents' house. When the song had run its course, the weather forecast came on the radio. Madison was pleased to note that the weekend promised to be warm and sunny, without even the slightest chance of rain. She kept the car rolling along the road, glancing now and again at the country scenery that was flying by the car windows. The time of year was early autumn, and the leaves that decorated the trees were just beginning to change colour. Most were still a vibrant green, but once in a while, Madison noticed some patches of deep burgundy. Sometimes there was a streak of dazzling orange thrown into the mix. The fall was her favourite season. Madison took a deep breath, letting it out slowly, enjoying the spectacular palette of colour that blanketed the countryside. As Madison steered the car around the next bend in the highway, she felt it jerk suddenly to the right. The sound of a flat tire reached her ears. She quickly pulled the car off the road, safely out of the way of the scurrying traffic. She reached over to wake up Ben. He slipped back to consciousness with a start, clutching his ribs in a protective manner. "Huh?" he mumbled sleepily. "Duty calls," Madison announced. "We've got a flat tire, so I guess you're not getting the day off after all." Ben moaned in discomfort. "I just ate," he complained. "Better get a move on," she told him. "We don't want to be late."

Madison stayed in the driver's seat while Ben got out. He went around to the back of the car and tried to find the jack and spare tire that were buried in the deep confines of the trunk. He quickly grabbed their overnight bags and transferred them to the backseat. With the luggage stowed safely out of his way, he had little trouble finding the jack and removing the spare tire from the bottom of the trunk. Leaning the spare against the car's bumper, Ben dug the tire iron out of the corner of the trunk and popped the cover off the rim. Next, he began loosening the lug nuts that held the wheel in place. Once all of the nuts had been broken free, he slid the small jack under the vehicle and started to crank it up. He continued cranking, raising the car until the flat tire was no longer touching the ground. Ben finished taking off the nuts in a flash, tossed the flat tire in the trunk, and slipped the spare onto the hub. He finger tightened the lug nuts as far as he could before lowering the jack and tightening them the rest of the way with the tire iron. Ben placed the tire iron and jack back into the trunk, pausing to examine the flat tire more closely. Turning it over, he noticed a sharp gash in the sidewall. He frowned darkly at the deflated rubber carcass, wondering how Madison had managed to ruin it in such a fashion. Ben thought about it for a moment longer. Then he decided he had better things to do than stand on the side of a busy highway staring at a useless hunk of rubber. Heaving a deep sigh, he shut the trunk and trudged back to the front of the car to rejoin Madison. She was waiting behind the wheel, drumming her fingers impatiently on the dash. "We're all set," Ben informed her. "Let's get out of here."

Once Madison had brought the car up to speed and slipped back into the flow of traffic, she took a glance at Ben. He was sitting beside her, staring off into the distance. "How bad was it?" she asked. "Will you be able to fix it?" Ben shook his head. "Nah, I doubt it. There was a big gouge in the sidewall. Even if I could, it's probably not worth fixing." Madison made a sour face. "Well, hopefully that's the only problem we have on this trip. I don't want to run into the same issues that we had last time we went to visit my parents." On their previous trip up north, they had been stranded on the side of the road for almost two hours waiting for a tow truck after the car's water pump had quit on them. They had been scorched by the blistering sun while they sat on the edge of the ditch, staring at the horizon, hoping to catch a glimpse of an approaching tow truck. Madison could still remember that miserable incident with stunning clarity. As she thought about it, she could almost feel the beads of sweat that had run down her face as she had waited on the shoulder of the busy road. Ben brought her back to reality with a simple question. "How much longer until we get there?" he asked impishly. Madison reached over and smacked him playfully on the side of the head.

"We'll get there when we get there," she answered. Ben slumped down in his seat and began to glare at his shoes. "You know I hate these long drives," he stated mournfully. Madison did her best to ignore him. "I get so uncomfortable being cramped up in this car for so long," Ben continued. "Why did we have to visit your parents this weekend?" Madison let out a long sigh. "Are you almost done whining?" she asked. "You're starting to sound like a little kid. You knew this was going to be a long drive, so just keep your complaints to yourself and try to enjoy it." Ben muttered something under his breath that Madison couldn't quite make out. She shook her head and kept the car moving. They continued along the highway in complete silence, with Madison palming the steering wheel, all the while keeping an eye on traffic. Ben was staring out the passenger side window, and suddenly seemed to have obtained a rather strong interest in every vehicle they were passing. Half an hour went by, and still neither one of them had said a word. Up ahead was a large sign advertising the next rest area to be only ten kilometres away. Finally, Madison broke the ice by announcing her intentions to pull into the rest area for a trip to the bathroom. A few minutes later, she guided the car to an off-ramp, which led them to a good-sized parking lot with a nice restroom beside it. Madison brought the car to a halt near the entrance of the building and ran in to use the toilet. Ben opened his door and slowly got to his feet. He stretched, trying to remove some of the stiffness that was plaguing his joints. While he waited for Madison to return, he paced around the car a couple of times until he felt somewhat better. Letting his impatient nature get the best of him, he slid his lanky frame into the driver's seat and sat there, tapping his foot on the floor and whistling through his teeth. As he waited, he began to wonder if there was some kind of colossal waiting line for the women's restroom. Ben turned the key in the ignition until the radio came to life. He began jabbing the seek button with his finger, trying to find music he liked. The first station he came to was a country station that was playing something entirely too slow for Ben's taste. As he sat there listening, he felt his eyelids begin to grow heavy. He flicked the key to the off position, bringing an end to the dreary music that had been lulling him to sleep. He was about to go looking for Madison, when she came jogging back over to the car with a couple cans of soda in her grasp. She raised an eyebrow when she saw him perched behind the wheel. "Did you want to drive?" she asked him. Ben shrugged. "Whatever's fastest," he replied casually. "You can if you want," Madison answered. "Just don't drive like an idiot. We're not in a race."

The car was scooting along on the far left side of the highway. Ben was doing his utmost to pass every vehicle in sight while trying to guzzle back his soda at the same time. Madison cocked her head to the side now and then to take a peek at the needle of the speedometer. In her opinion, the needle was resting quite a bit farther to the right than she liked. Ben kept ploughing along, weaving through traffic without using his signals, not wanting to be delayed for even an instant. When they got to the top of the next hill, Madison suddenly yelled, "Cop!" Ben hammered on the brakes, making a frantic dive for the slow lane. "Where?" he asked her quickly. Scanning the approaching shoulders of the road, he could spot nothing. He glanced over at Madison and was surprised to see her laughing so hard she was almost in tears. "You're unbelievable," he muttered.

Looking for Work

Ben was kneeling on the ground next to a dual-axle float trailer. The county's road works department had dropped it off at his shop the day before. Each of the float's two axles had four tires, and it was his intention to replace all of them. Although most of the lug nuts seemed to be fairly rusted, Ben found that they were easily removed with his pneumatic wrench. He whistled a rather cheerful tune as he worked away on the float. It was a warm October day. The bright sun was beating down on him, but the gentle breeze that fluttered about made it quite enjoyable. Ben loved the feel of a pleasant autumn day. Everything felt so crisp and fresh.

It didn't take him long to remove all eight wheels from the float, and his next step was to go off in search of the forklift that he knew was hiding somewhere in the shop. As he walked through the bay door, located in the back wall of the shop, Ben spotted the forklift tucked away in a corner. There was a pallet of tires on the forks, and some assorted tools and dirty shop rags were strewn across the seat, giving Ben the impression that someone had been working on the machine. He frowned, wondering what could be wrong with the forklift this time. "Tim!" he hollered. "Where are you?" The sound of muffled footsteps could be heard on the upper level of the shop, trampling through the storage room and thundering down the stairs. A second later, Tim appeared, panting and out of breath. "What's up?" he gasped. "Were you working on the forklift?" Ben questioned him. "Oh, yeah," he replied. "I just changed the oil and checked the tire pressure. I took a peek at the brake fluid level also, because the other day I couldn't stop. It looks like the reservoir is just about dry, so I picked up some new brake fluid. I didn't have a chance to fill up the reservoir yet." Ben nodded thoughtfully. "Maybe there's a slow leak somewhere," he wondered. "There might be," Tim agreed. "Why don't I just fill it up?" he suggested. "Then we can run it for a while and see what happens." "Good," said Ben. "Why don't you go ahead with that, and when you're done, bring the forklift outside. I've got a bunch of rims waiting for new tires out there." "You're the boss," said Tim. "I'll get right on it." Ben grinned. "Perfect," he said, turning around and heading back outside. On his way out, he grabbed an empty pallet from a stack in the back corner of the shop. He dragged it behind him over to the float and began piling the wheels on top of it. He had just placed the last tire on the pallet when he heard a voice coming from behind him. "Excuse me, sir." Turning around, he saw a somewhat nervous looking boy of about sixteen years old standing there. He had light brown hair and glasses and was wearing a faded red T-shirt and blue jeans. "What can I help you with?" Ben asked him pleasantly. "My name is Patrick," the boy stated. "I was hoping that you might have a job for me. You know, just for after school." Ben thought about it for a moment. "Possibly," he answered. "Do you have any experience, Patrick?" Patrick looked downcast for a second. "Not really," he admitted slowly, "But I'm a fast learner." "No experience at all?" Ben inquired. "What about a bicycle? You've probably changed a flat tire on a bicycle before, haven't you?" Patrick's expression brightened considerably. "Actually, yeah," he said excitedly. "I have changed a few bike tires before." Ben laughed. "So you do have *some* experience," he said. "Yeah, I guess so," agreed Patrick. "Good," Ben replied. "Never sell yourself short."

As Patrick stood there in front of him, his bright blue eyes wide with excitement, Ben found it almost uncanny how much the young kid reminded him of himself at that age. When he was a teenager, before he began working for his uncle at the tire shop, he would take whatever work was offered to him. While he was standing there, he began reminiscing, mentally listing off all the different jobs he had held over the course of his school years. His first year of high school, his summer job had been on a berry farm, just around the corner from his house. Each day he was given a small basket that he could fit three quart-sized containers into. Then he would wander up and down the endless rows of raspberries, picking a handful at a time. Most of the handfuls of delicious red berries made it into his basket, but some days, he supposed, he must have eaten almost as many as he had turned in. It had been a great job—he loved being outside all day in the fresh air and could snack to his heart's content. Eventually though, after he had come home from work more than once with a severe case of the runs, Ben's mother had insisted that he stop eating so much of the ripened produce. He reluctantly had agreed.

The following summer, his place of employment was with a different farm, a couple of side roads over. Ben had ridden his bicycle to work every morning until he finally managed to convince his dad to let him take the family four-wheeler. His dad had only granted him permission on the condition that he went straight there and back. It had really been something, cruising along the gravel side roads on the little machine. Ben had felt so free and independent. Unfortunately, it had been a short-lived joy, much to his shame. As he rode back and forth to work each day, he had noticed an entrance to a trail calling out to him from the edge of the woods along the road. The trail had piqued his curiosity, and he had often wondered where it might lead him. On a steamy summer day after work, as he was making his way back home, he turned the four-wheeler off the road and began exploring the trail. It had been great fun, with lots of hills to manoeuvre and a few fallen trees to climb over. By the time Ben had reached a small creek that meandered through the middle of the trail, he was in his glory. The creek looked fairly shallow, so Ben put his machine in four-wheel drive and took a run at it. He was almost halfway across before he realized his mistake. The water was considerably deeper than he had first thought. He quickly had to jump on top of the seat to avoid getting wet, the ends of his handlebars just barely sticking above the surface of the water. Ben barely made it across. The four-wheeler almost died on him as it emerged from the water on the other side of the creek. He kept moving along the trail, and five minutes later, was dismayed to find himself back at the creek. Ben looked around but couldn't find any other route that might have afforded him an easier crossing. He took a deep breath and hit the throttle. The four-wheeler ploughed through the creek, spraying water in every direction. Just like the first time, Ben hardly managed to get to the other side without stalling the machine. Once he was through the creek, he hurried to get back out to the road. The four-wheeler seemed kind of sluggish as he retraced his path. As he attempted to climb the first steep hill, he got most of the way up before he found out why. The drive belt on the machine had gotten wet when he rode through the creek, and now it was slipping. Ben hit the gas a little harder and was able to reach the top of the hill. Luckily, the rest of the trail was fairly open from there on out, and he was able to maintain a healthy speed, enabling him to make it back to the road. By the time Ben got home, the belt was finally dried out and performing as normal. When he pulled the muddy four-wheeler into the laneway, his dad was waiting for him, wondering why he was so late. And why the four-wheeler was so dirty. The next day, Ben was pedaling to work.

The year after that, Ben had been employed by a landscaping company. The company ran two different crews: one that carried out the construction aspect of the business, and another, which Ben worked on, that took care of maintenance. If he had to choose, this particular job probably would have been his favourite. He didn't mind working in the blazing sun all day. And he loved flying around on one of the company's riding mowers. Ben had worked long hours all summer long, hoping to save enough money to buy a snowmobile the coming winter. Actually, to be technical, Ben hadn't worked long hours *all* summer. Nearly two weeks before he was to return to school, he had decided to quit his job. His heart just hadn't been in it any longer. When he thought about what had happened, he sometimes still felt a little queasy. There had been an elderly lady whose lawn Ben had cut every week. The old lady had a small poodle named Snowball. Usually, the dog was kept inside the house whenever the lawn was being cut, but on this particular day, the little pooch had gotten out and was prancing about the yard. This house was the last one on their to-do list for the day, and Ben, along with the rest of the crew, was in a hurry to finish up and get home. As Ben piloted the riding mower around the corner of the house, Snowball had jumped out of the flower bed and right into the path of the spinning blade. He never had a chance. All Ben heard was a muffled yelp and then a dull thud. The exhaust note the mower was producing slowed for a moment before picking up again as the mower continued on its path. Glancing behind him, Ben was horrified with the sight that met his eyes. The little poodle that had, only moments earlier, been so animated and lifelike, was now lying in a mangled heap on the grass. He felt so sick to his stomach that he went to the truck and waited for the rest of the guys to finish with the yard. Ben had nightmares for weeks afterward, and was still able to picture clearly the old lady's face when she realized what had happened to her beloved Snowball.

The sound of Tim approaching on the forklift snapped Ben back to the present. Patrick was still standing in front of him, hands in his pockets, eagerly waiting for a response. Ben looked him in the eye for a moment. Then he offered Patrick his hand. "When can you start?"

Printed in the United States
151206LV00001B/1/P